Praise for

OVE, LIES AND LEMON PIE

"A delight, delicious and feather-light YA romance that
still manages to deal beautifully with some deep issues."
Robin Stevens, author of MURDER MOST UNLADYLIKE

"Emotionally charged YA romance"
LoveReading4Kids

"Cannon has a light touch and the result is delicious.
The friendships feel real, the situations authentic.
Teen girls will devour this, and come back for more."
Books for Keeps

"A perfect sunshine read for all recipe and
romance fans. Baking is the new craze sweeping
across the country and this tasty, teasing tale of a girl
with a family secret who finds solace in cake-making
presses all the right chocolate buttons."
Lancashire Evening Post

"Thoroughly entertaining and filled with many
heart-warming moments, *Love, Lies and Lemon Pies*
delivers in every way!"
Book Passion for Life

"*Love, Lies and Lemon Pies* is a delicious young adult
contemporary novel to devour."
Pretty Books

And THEN we RAN

For Mum and Dad
At least I never ran off to Gretna Green...

STRIPES PUBLISHING
An imprint of the Little Tiger Group
1 The Coda Centre, 189 Munster Road, London SW6 6AW

A paperback original
First published in Great Britain in 2017

ISBN: 978-1-84715-799-7

Text copyright © Katy Cannon, 2017
Cover copyright © Stripes Publishing Ltd, 2017
Cover images © shutterstock.com and Maskot/Getty Images (girl's top).

And THEN we RAN

Stripes

Megan

The day I lost my virginity was the day I lost my sister.

The guy – Dylan – doesn't matter, not any more. He was a mistake from start to finish. But not nearly as much of a mistake as not being on the beach with Lizzie that night.

Lizzie was the golden girl of our family – always happy, always top of the class, always kind and thoughtful and hardly ever sulky. Mum used to say it was like she wasn't a teenager at all. She had a few really close friends – the sort of friends our parents approved of. She took part in school activities, was set to be head girl for her final year and was applying to Oxbridge. She knew exactly what she wanted to be when she grew up – a lawyer, like Mum and Dad, but specializing in human rights. She was a dream daughter.

I was basically the opposite of all that.

My whole life, I'd been compared to Lizzie and found lacking. At least, by my parents. And my teachers. And anyone over the age of about twenty-two. I had no ambition, no focus, no self-discipline. I jumped from one idea, one hobby, one boyfriend, one dream to the next and never settled on anything.

And OK, they might have had a point. I would probably never excel academically but I knew how to make people like me and how to get them on my side. And that, I decided, was a skill in itself.

I figured I'd spend my whole life not being quite as good as Lizzie. Being the screw-up little sister, the one who always needed bailing out after her latest wild idea.

Until suddenly Lizzie wasn't there for me to be compared to any more.

It was over a year since her death and I still hadn't got used to it. Hadn't accepted that our last-ever conversation was her telling me I was making another mistake – that Dylan wasn't worth it, that I was too young. Hadn't got over the fact that she was right. And that if I'd listened to her, just for once, Lizzie might still be here to tell me when I was screwing up.

But she wasn't.

It sounds stupid but the whole thing started with a selfie. One spur-of-the-moment photo that made me realize I was now older than my big sister.

I held my phone out at arm's length, camera screen facing me, and angled it to try and get both my face and the top I was trying on into the picture. Since I was standing in the cramped changing cubicle upstairs at Oracle, the New Age shop where my best friend Becca worked part-time, it wasn't all that easy. Neither of us have lessons on a Friday afternoon so, as Year 13 students, we're allowed to head home at lunchtime, supposedly to study in peace. Becca spends Friday afternoons covering for her boss, Lily-Ann, at Oracle. I usually spend them annoying Becca.

Eventually I had the shot framed and took the photo. The phone made its fake camera shutter noise, the screen went black for a second, then the photo popped up again, flipped from the mirror image I'd seen when I was composing it to show the real me, not my reflection.

I stared at it, my heart thumping too hard, until the camera screen returned.

I look like Lizzie.

My legs wobbled and I dropped down to sit on the floor, pressing the screen to bring up the photo again.

I'm usually the one behind the camera, not in front of it. I wouldn't even have taken the selfie except that Becca wanted to see what the top looked like on and it seemed easier than traipsing all the way back downstairs to show her, and risking the wrath of Lily-Ann, who'd stopped in en route to the bank. (Lily-Ann usually stayed as far away from the shop as possible, which was why she'd hired Becca. But when she did pop in she always complained about me hanging around and messing up the stock.)

As I stared at the photo, I reached up to touch my face, running my fingers against the cheekbones that suddenly felt higher, more prominent. Even my hair was just like hers used to be – long and blond and a mess of waves and kinks.

Lizzie had been seventeen and seven weeks old when she died, a year and a bit older than me. I'd turned seventeen in August, three whole months ago. Last month, I'd officially become older than she ever would be – and I'd missed it. I'd missed that split second where things changed. I hadn't even noticed that every day I grew more like her.

Was this what my parents saw when they looked

at me? Did they see me, Megan, at all? Or was I just a Lizzie replacement failing to live up to the memory of the daughter they'd lost?

It would certainly explain a lot.

Footsteps thundered up the stairs and Becca pulled open the curtain and peered in. "Lily-Ann's gone off to the bank. Come on, get up and let me see!"

"I don't think I like it," I said, standing. Actually I had no idea what the top looked like but there wasn't a chance in hell of my buying it now.

Becca eyed me up and down. "Yeah, no. It's not really you."

What *was* me? I'd thought I knew exactly who I was – now I wasn't sure at all.

"Right." I stripped the top off and pulled my jumper back on, pushing past Becca and out into the shop. The top floor of Oracle was all clothes – mostly floaty ones with tie-dye patterns – and accessories, like woven hemp bags. Downstairs was where the tarot cards, dreamcatchers and angel figurines lived. Without waiting for Becca, I headed back down the stairs.

Lizzie would never have missed a single anniversary if I'd been the one who hadn't come home from that boat ride. From now on, every moment I lived would be one she never got. Every day, every year, every birthday, every milestone…

It was like I had to live them for both of us, now. My skin felt too tight, all of a sudden, like there wasn't room for me *and* Lizzie inside it. "You OK, Meg?" Becca frowned at me from the top of the stairs and I tried to shake off the feelings coursing through me. There was nothing Becca could do or say to make it better.

"I'm fine," I lied. Maybe I'd talk to her about it, once I'd thought it through a bit more. Ask whether she saw Lizzie when she looked at me. What she thought Lizzie would say about my life. Whether she thought I'd spend my whole life trying to live up to someone who wasn't even there any more.

But not yet.

"OK." Becca still looked suspicious, but she let it go. "How was the gallery? Did Elodie like your portfolio?"

My portfolio. My photos. I'd almost forgotten about them.

When Lizzie died, her memory had consumed every moment. The therapist my parents sent me to had suggested I find something else to fill that space. A distraction, or a new focus, I guess. So I'd taken up photography and finally discovered the one thing I loved so much I couldn't imagine doing anything else.

The one thing I could commit to.

Which was why Elodie's rejection stung so much. I'd decided to use my free afternoon productively for once, and taken my A level photography portfolio down to the Seashell Gallery as soon as classes finished to see if any of the photos might be good enough for Elodie, the owner, to display and sell.

"She said no." I settled myself on to the stool beside the counter, while Becca stood behind it. It wasn't like there'd be any customers in, but Becca took her job seriously. She'd be lucky if more than a handful of tourists even came into the shop between now and Easter, and most of the locals weren't that interested in dreamcatchers.

"Just no?" Becca asked. "But your photos are great! I love your seaside ones."

I shrugged. "Oh, she said some of them were OK. Just 'not a fit for the Seashell Gallery'." Which, since quite a few of them were still lifes of actual seashells, seemed like a very polite way of saying 'Hell no, not in a million years, you suck'. "She liked this one, though." I dug into my portfolio case, pulled out the photo in question and handed it to Becca.

It was taken at the beach, same as the others I'd shown Elodie, but this one included people. I'd taken it around the fire one Friday night during the summer, in the small, secret cove where all the local teenagers tended to gather – and which the police pretended they didn't know about. It was far enough from the tourist beaches that we didn't really bother anyone and we were probably better at clearing up after ourselves than a lot of the visitors anyway. After all, this was *our* beach.

In the photo, Becca is laughing in the fire's glow, the sparks and heat warming up her skin, her tightly coiled black hair gleaming under the moonlight. Becca could be a model – like, she was actually approached by scouts when we were shopping in the city one day. But Becca wants to be a marine biologist. (I've suggested she could do both but she says that posing for me is enough of a job, thanks.)

Across from her sit Elliott and Sean Redwood. Sean's mouth is half open – probably telling the joke that made Becca laugh. Behind them, you can see the movement of other bodies, all streaks in the starlight, dancing on the sand, waves rippling behind them. Everything is in motion except for Elliott, who sits still and steady beside Sean. Looking at the photo, it was harder than ever to imagine that Elliott and I had been best friends once. Especially since we'd barely spoken two words to each other since the day after Lizzie died.

But Becca wasn't looking at the photo to see Elliott.

I watched, waiting for a reaction, as she ran her finger along the edge of the print, not quite touching the image of Sean's face, but close. I'd never shown her this photo before but I was certain she'd remember the night it was taken.

"Did you hear, by the way?" Becca handed the photo back to me, her hands moving immediately to straighten a stack of tarot card boxes on the counter. "*Someone* is back in town."

"Would this *someone* be tall, dark and wearing a Navy uniform?" I asked, eyebrows raised.

"He doesn't actually wear the uniform yet, but in principle … yeah."

Sean Redwood. Becca's first and only one-night stand, over the summer. Shortly afterwards he'd left town, but given how much Becca had talked about him over the last few months, it was like he'd never gone away.

Sean was a couple of years ahead of us at school and his younger brother Elliott was in our year. I'd known them my whole life, more or less. Ever since we moved in next door to them when I was three, anyway. They'd moved across town when I was eleven, but St Evaline wasn't that big and us locals all knew the ins and outs of everyone's lives.

To be honest, I was getting a bit bored of Becca going on about Sean. I couldn't remember him ever sticking with one girl for more than a fortnight.

Becca knew this as well as I did, even though her family had only moved to town when she was twelve. But still, she hoped. Becca was incurably optimistic about life in general. Normally, I felt obliged to point out the reality of the situation.

But I'd had enough reality for one day. Encouraging Becca to actually *do* something about her crush sounded like the perfect distraction.

"He's on leave?" I asked, digging for the details.

"Just home for the weekend." Becca rolled her eyes. "He's not actually in the Navy yet, Meg. He's at uni on a Navy scholarship. It's a different thing."

"Yeah, well, I haven't exactly kept up on the particulars of his career the way you have, you know…" I leaned over and bumped her shoulder with my own. "So? He's back. What are you going to do about it?" Optimism without action got you nowhere at all and I couldn't stand the thought of Becca moping over him until he came home for Christmas.

"Do?" Becca's eyes grew comically big.

"Yeah," I said. "Like, text him or call him." I jumped up as a flash of genius struck me. "In fact, you need to text Sean right now and ask him if he's going to be at the beach tonight!" It was Friday night and the opportunities for fun were kind of limited in St Evaline. If Sean was home, chances were good he'd be down the beach, along with everyone else we knew. "I already told Tyler and Ewan we'd be there, and Rosie, Sophia and Emily are meeting us, too. Sean *has* to come."

"I'm not sure..." Becca started.

"I am." I reached across and grabbed her phone from her back pocket. A few keystrokes later and it was mission accomplished. "Done!" I said, handing it back. "Now, I need to go home and figure out what to wear tonight." There was a fine line between warmth and hotness when dressing for parties on the beach in winter. "Meet you there at eight?"

Becca nodded, still staring at the phone in her hand. I grinned at her, then pushed away from the counter and headed out.

Distraction achieved. Now I just needed to focus on having fun, without dwelling on the fact that my sister wasn't there to share it with me.

Elliott

November in St Evaline is grim. Icy winds gusting in across the Irish Sea, constant rain, and it's too cold to even go surfing. Basically, by the time we hit November, I'm just holding out for spring again.

There are some good things about living here – my mates, my girlfriend Amy, Mum, the sea, the boats ... and that's about it.

The list of bad things is masses longer – the fact that the whole town hates my dad, the fact that *I* hate my dad, the fact that the whole town hates *me* ... and that's just for starters. But it doesn't make any difference. St Evaline is home and it's likely where I'll be stuck for the rest of my life, so I have to make the best of it.

But as I watched the four lads crossing the sand, I knew this was one of those days where the bad things eclipsed the good completely. It seemed that a timetabling quirk meant that most Year 13s had free periods on Friday afternoons

– probably because the teachers knew there was a solid chance we wouldn't show up anyway. But I really wished these four, in particular, were stuck in some boring lesson right now, instead of being here on my beach.

Ducking my head, I went back to scrubbing down the boat I was working on – one of the smaller boats, which we use for the seal safaris and smugglers' cave trips. Although the weather was getting worse and half-term was over, we still had the occasional tourist stopping by at the weekends. And even if we didn't, Iestyn, who owned the boats, would make me spend my free Friday afternoons cleaning them anyway. Just in case.

Right now, I was glad of the work. Focusing on the boat meant I could ignore the company headed my way. If I got really lucky, they might not notice me at all. Unlikely.

"Look who it is, boys." I recognized the voice without even looking up. Dylan Roberts, the younger brother of Evan Roberts. Good Welsh boys from a good local family. At least, that's what they'd have people believe. The Roberts family were as beloved in town as the Redwoods were hated.

"Elliott Redwood," Dylan said, leaning in closer until it was impossible to ignore him. "The boy who ruined my brother's life."

I knew I should just ignore him but I couldn't help it. "At least he still has a life," I muttered.

Because Lizzie didn't. And that was at least partly Evan's fault, as far as I was concerned.

Of course, it was also partly mine. But I was paying my penance, too, wasn't I?

Dylan's friends made the sort of noises that suggested I'd started something, egging him on to retaliate. Great. Just what I didn't want.

The thing was, it was over a year since Lizzie died, and six months since the trial ended, but nobody in St Evaline was moving on. Just like they'd never moved on from what my dad did, even once he was tried, convicted and locked up. It didn't matter that I hadn't spoken to him since he got put away or that I was just as mad at him as the rest of the town. Dad had stolen the town's money, embezzling the funds his construction company should have been using to improve St Evaline and make it more attractive to tourists. That was his legacy. And I was his son – so with him gone, all the hatred the people felt towards him was heaped on me instead.

At least I'd actually done the things Dylan and Evan hated me for.

"I bet you got just what you wanted, didn't you?" Dylan's cheeks were flushed and I couldn't tell if it was from the wind or his anger. I straightened up, ready to take whatever he wanted to throw at me this time. "You were so jealous of Evan and the rest of us, you had to screw up his life until it was as crap as yours."

Evan had got a two-year Youth Rehabilitation Order for stealing the boat – he didn't even get locked up. His solicitor had argued that he was a valued member of the school community with a bright future ahead of him, that he'd never stepped out of line before and had shown genuine distress and remorse for what happened that night. Besides, Lizzie had been drunk and the other guys on the boat swore she jumped off. It was just bad luck that she hit her head.

Bad luck. Bad luck and two years of best behaviour for Evan.

It made me sick to think about it.

One of Dylan's mates, Freddie, laughed. "Come on, Dyl. Redwood's life is still crapper. Right?"

"True." Dylan leaned in closer, until I could almost smell his breath. "But if this tosser hadn't stuck his nose into stuff that wasn't his business, Evan wouldn't have had to go to court. He wouldn't have a record. It's his fault Ev didn't get into uni."

"Or it could just be because he's thick," I said, staring Dylan down.

I wasn't going to let them think they could drive me out. Whatever I'd done, whatever Dad had done, this was my home. And you know what? I'd done the right thing, whatever Dylan thought. And if I were in the same situation, I'd do it again.

I'd spent the last year avoiding the Roberts family as best I could. But I couldn't avoid them forever. It was time to stand up and own my actions.

Of course, I was pretty sure standing up was about to get me thrashed.

Just another part of my penance for not saving Lizzie.

Megan

The string of tiny golden bells hanging from the doorframe jingled as I left Oracle. Outside the autumn air blew in cold off the sea and I wrapped my jacket tighter around me as I crossed back through the small town centre. The place was pretty much empty; during term times the only people left were the locals, and there were less of us every year. Most of the pretty coloured cottages on the seafront were holiday homes now. Even my parents and I lived out past the train station, in a normal red-brick house.

The wind whipped past me, blowing me towards home, but I couldn't make myself hurry. I walked slowly along the seafront, pausing by the metal railing separating the pavement from the rocky bank that led down to the sand below. The metal was cold through my jacket as I rested my arms against it, taking out my phone and pulling up the photo I'd taken in the changing room.

This time, I just saw a picture of me. Same old face, same old hair. Chewing on my bottom lip, I scrolled through to my favourites folder and pulled up an older shot – one that I'd transferred when I upgraded my phone at the start of the year. The one photo I always wanted to have with me.

In it, Lizzie and I are leaning against the same railing I was at now, the sea behind us and the sun in front, turning our hair golden and our skin bright. She stands a few of centimetres taller than me, just-turned-seventeen to my almost sixteen. It was the last photo I had of my sister.

I pressed the button on the side of my phone and made the screen go black, staring out at the waves crashing against the harbour. The boats further out were just starting to bob on the incoming tide while those higher up the beach were still grounded. I frowned as I spotted a small group of boys around one of the boats.

Dylan. Freddie. Harry and Rob. And behind them … Elliott.

I tensed as I watched, fairly sure that any gathering that involved Dylan and Elliott being in the same place at the same time couldn't be a good idea.

In a town as small as St Evaline, it was impossible not to know what had happened to Elliott since the trial. He'd been enough of an outcast before Lizzie's death, thanks to his father's screw-ups. But since he spoke out against Evan and the others at the trial, he'd basically been shunned by the whole town: even those who hadn't been willing to condemn him for his dad's actions couldn't forgive him for bringing down Evan Roberts. St Evaline looks after its own.

Except Elliott was the only person who'd been looking after Lizzie that night. Even if he hadn't been able to save her.

I owed Elliott an apology. I'd owed it to him for six months already but admitting I was wrong wasn't very me, and since Elliott and I didn't really talk any more anyway … it had been so much easier to say nothing.

But today Lizzie seemed to be all around me. So maybe this was the day to make my apologies to Elliott and move on. Accept that I was older now than Lizzie would ever be, that I didn't have the memory of her at my age to fail to live up to any more. Begin living in a post-Lizzie world.

Starting with Elliott.

I glanced down again and saw Dylan looming over Elliott as he was backed up against the boat. God, and

I'd let that idiot actually *touch* me once. What the hell had I been thinking?

Dylan pulled back his fist.

Definitely time to interrupt.

Leaning out over the railings, I put my fingers in my mouth and whistled, the way Elliott had taught me to when we were seven.

The sound cut through the air, sharp and shrill, just as I'd intended, and I waited for them to turn round and notice me.

Elliott

Dylan grabbed my shoulders and threw me back against the boat, sending the air flying from my body. I gasped, desperately trying to catch my breath before Dylan's raised fist hit, when suddenly I heard a high-pitched whistle.

I knew that sound. I looked up and saw Megan Hughes leaning over the railings above the beach, her hair blowing everywhere in the wind.

Dylan and his mates spun round, obviously expecting to find someone official approaching. Instead they saw Megan sauntering down the steps on to the sand.

"That got your attention, huh?" She was smiling – a wide, friendly smile although it seemed like there might be something else behind it. Six years ago I'd have known for sure. But ever since I'd moved house at the age of eleven, Megan and I had drifted further and further apart.

The morning the coastguard brought Lizzie's body in, any connection we'd had left was severed for good.

"What do you want, Megan?" Dylan snapped, his face still red.

He and Megan had gone out, once. I had no idea what ended it, though, or what sort of terms they were on now. To be honest, it used to be hard to keep up with Megan's boyfriends. But she and Dylan had dated for months, up until Lizzie's death. They must have broken up somewhere in the aftermath. And since then… Well, I hadn't seen her with any guys at all, really.

Megan kept her tone light as she answered. "I was just checking you were planning on being down the cove tonight."

"Course. Where else would we be?" Freddie asked.

"Great. In that case, maybe you could get me something to drink later?" She pulled her purse out of her school bag and extracted a ten-pound note, holding it out with a smile.

Dylan's answering smile was slow, like he was just realizing something important. Dylan was still only seventeen, same as Megan. Freddie, on the other hand, had turned eighteen last month and the supermarket tended to turn a blind eye to how much booze he bought on a Friday night.

Except it wasn't Freddie who took the money. It was Dylan. "Course. The usual?" My skin crawled at the idea of Dylan knowing Megan's favourite drink when I no longer did. It used to be a forbidden lemonade at the ice-cream parlour, because she wasn't allowed fizzy drinks at home.

"Yes, please." She rested a hand on his arm, briefly. "See you there."

And then she waited.

It took Dylan a moment to catch on, possibly still blinded by Megan's smile. But eventually he said, "Come on then, lads. Not wasting any more time here." He shot me a filthy look. I smiled back blandly.

Megan held off until they'd disappeared up the stone steps to the town above and then she shuddered.

"Urgh. Now I'm going to have to be nice to him for at least five minutes tonight to get my drink." She turned and pointed a finger at me. "You owe me, Redwood."

"You didn't have to interfere," I observed. "Wait, so you weren't actually flirting with Dylan?"

"God, no." She rolled her eyes. "He was about to beat you up, Elliott."

"So?" There were plenty who would say I deserved it. Until that moment, I hadn't been sure whether Megan was one of them.

How could you, Elliott? How could you let her go with them? Her words the morning after Lizzie's death still echoed around my brain sometimes, late at night. A reminder of all the things I'd got wrong.

"So, if I'd had to drag you to the hospital to have your face put back together, I might have forgotten to apologize," she said.

I blinked, trying to follow her train of thought. I was out of practice at Megan-speak and the way she jumped topics faster than shoals of fish changed direction.

"Apologize for what?" I asked.

Megan pulled the cuffs of her jumper over her hands, curling her fingers up into woolly fists. "For what I said that morning. After they found Lizzie." She looked up, met my gaze, and there, behind the make-up, was the ten-year-old girl who'd been my best friend in the world. "I shouldn't have blamed you. It wasn't your fault."

"What changed your mind?" I didn't know what else to say. Because she was wrong – in lots of ways it was my fault. I *should* have stopped Evan from taking the boat out that night. Trying wasn't enough. I'd failed and Lizzie had died.

"Hearing your testimony at the trial."

"Six months ago."

Megan shrugged.

"Right." What had happened, I wondered, to make her come and talk to me today? Was it seeing Dylan and the others about to beat me up? Or was there something else going on?

"I'll see you at the cove tonight?" she asked.

"Maybe. It might be a good night to steer clear." I wasn't sure I could face it. Sure, my friends would be there. But everyone else would be, too. Including Dylan, with Megan's drinks, and maybe even his brother.

"You should come," Megan said fiercely. "Don't let them— You did the right thing, Elliott. Don't let them pretend otherwise."

I knew I'd done the right thing. But hearing Megan say it... "OK. Maybe."

"Good." She bounced a little on her toes, always too wired with energy to stay still for long. "I'll save you a drink."

She turned and took a few steps up the beach, away from the harbour. Then she stopped and spun back again, a frown creasing her forehead, only just visible in the gloomy afternoon light. "Elliott?"

"Yeah?"

"Do you think I look like her? Like Lizzie, I mean?"

My breath caught, as I remembered her sister asking me almost the same question, that last night. *Don't you think I look like her, Elliott? I'm as pretty as Megan, right?*

I'd never told Megan that part of the story. Never told anyone.

And half an hour later, Lizzie had climbed into that boat with Evan Roberts.

I swallowed and tried to find the right words to answer her.

"I think you look like you," I called out finally, as she walked away.

Exactly like I'd said to Lizzie.

Megan

Both my parents' cars were in the driveway when I reached the house. That in itself was weird; it was only just four, although the daylight was almost gone. Normally Mum and/or Dad would be working late, or at a client dinner, or travelling. They'd got shift-parenting down to a fine art when Lizzie and I were kids and it was worse now there was only one child to come home to. To have them both back so early was definitely not normal.

To walk into the house and find them sitting on the sofa together in the lounge was downright unnerving. The last time I remembered that happening was the day we got the call from the coastguard.

I'm so sorry, Mr and Mrs Hughes. It's your daughter. It's Lizzie.

The hardest thing in a town this size is that everyone knows everyone else's business. Over a year on, I could see Lizzie's death in every set of eyes that met mine. *Oh yes, Megan, the girl whose sister died.* Today she seemed closer than ever – especially after my conversation with Elliott on the beach.

Pushing the memories aside, I tossed my bag at the bottom of the stairs and headed in to find out what was going on. No point putting off the inevitable.

Maybe they were getting a divorce. Except since this was the first time I'd seen them in the same room for about a month, I had no idea when they'd have had time to decide that.

I threw myself on to the opposite sofa, displacing the cat, and tried not to stare at the framed photo on the side table – the one showing Lizzie in her school blazer and tie, smiling sweetly for the class photographer. "What's up?"

They looked at each other, communicating silently in that way couples seem to learn. Then Dad spoke. "I had a call from your college today."

Ah. That. Considerably less of a tragedy than last time, then. But still enough to get my parents in the same room.

"Really? What did they say?" No point giving away everything if the stupid college secretary hadn't.

"That you missed the Oxbridge application deadline

and now you're saying that you don't plan to apply to university at all. That you've asked to drop your law A level."

Damn. In my head, I'd sort of figured on having time to convince my parents that it was a good idea before it became a thing. Guess the college didn't get that memo. "Yeah. Well, I just thought—"

"Seems to me you didn't think at all," Mum interrupted, and Dad shot her a look. Her lips pursed up into a knot. I knew that expression and it was rarely good. "Look, we agreed at the beginning of the last school year that if you wanted to take photography, you'd have to study academic A levels and general studies, too. History, English and law."

"I *do* know which courses I'm taking, Mum," I snarked back. Dad sighed. When I first took up photography, they thought it was a great idea – as a hobby. They'd even bought me some glossy oversized books filled with photos of places I'd never heard of. But once it became clear that photography was a bigger priority for me than school or university, they'd gone off the whole thing. "Besides, *we* didn't decide anything. I said I wanted to take the full-time photography two-year diploma and you said no." And since the college agreed with them, I was somehow enrolled on the A level courses *they* wanted before I could even argue back. It was a miracle I'd been able to sneak in photography A level along with the ones my parents chose.

"We all agreed that academic A levels would stand you in better stead for your long-term career options than a limited vocational course," Dad said, mediating as usual. "But your marks aren't great, either, your tutor says. If you want to get into a good university—"

"And what if I don't?" It seemed like we'd been having this argument all year and they still weren't listening to me. "What if all I want is to get out of this town and start my career as a photographer? How is a law A level going to help me then?" Apart from anything else, I was failing it. I hadn't applied to Oxford or Cambridge because I knew I didn't stand a chance, even if I wanted it. But my parents wanted to believe I did … and suddenly I thought I knew why.

They'd never talked about my future – about university, about Oxbridge – before Lizzie died. It had been expected that Lizzie would be the family success story and I'd follow along doing whatever I liked.

But this last year, my future was all they'd seemed to think about. What I was going to do next, now Lizzie wasn't here to do it first. Maybe none of us had moved on from Lizzie's death at all. Maybe my parents had just transferred all the hopes and dreams they'd had for their perfect elder daughter on to me, the imperfect one. They wanted me to go to Oxbridge because that's where Lizzie had planned to go. How had I not seen that before?

"You're seventeen," Mum said, using the extraordinarily patronizing tone she saved for conversations about my future. "How can you possibly know now what you want for the rest of your life?"

"A degree opens doors," Dad added. "We're just trying to encourage you to keep your options open." He made it sound like he was the good cop to Mum's bad cop but, actually, they were both saying exactly the same thing: *We know better than you do.*

I shook my head. This wasn't their choice to make.

"When are you going to accept that I'm not the academic type?" *That I'm not Lizzie.* "University isn't for everyone, you know."

"Don't be stupid," Mum snapped. "Of course you're going to university. Your sister—"

"I'm *not* my sister." The words came out like whiplash. "I know Lizzie wanted to go. I know Lizzie had top marks and universities would have been fighting over her. But I'm not Lizzie."

Even Lizzie wasn't Lizzie any more. She was gone.

And she'd taken all that brightness with her. All that talent, all those brains. The future she might have had.

Except my parents were trying to cram all those things into *my* future instead. It wasn't enough for them that I looked like her. Now I had to *be* her, too. That feeling I'd had in Oracle smothered me again – the sense of trying to be everything all at once, Lizzie *and* Megan. I couldn't do it.

"Of course you're not," Dad said, his voice calm. "Nobody thinks you are."

"All I was going to say was that Lizzie would have jumped at the chances we're giving you," Mum said, making it clear that not only was Lizzie smarter, more talented and generally better than me, she was also more appreciative.

"If I'm so ungrateful anyway, maybe I should just drop out completely." I felt too hot, like something was burning inside me, fighting to get out. "Move to London and find a college that will actually let me study what I want, while I start building up my portfolio."

I wanted to be a photographer, travelling to places I hadn't even heard of yet, taking photos of the scenery and sending them home. London was the perfect base for being a creative – and most importantly, it was miles and miles away from Pembrokeshire, my parents and even Lizzie's memory.

"And live where?" Mum asked, her voice approaching a yell. "And on what? Don't imagine for a moment that we'll be supporting you."

I shrugged. I could find a job and work on my photography at night and on weekends. London was a photogenic city – I could build a great portfolio there. Better than seascapes, anyway. Something that would get me an in somewhere, persuade someone to give me a chance.

It would be a hell of a lot harder without my parents' money and support, but still. I might not have a plan, yet, but I had options.

"I'll have Grandma Alice's flat soon enough," I reminded them. She'd left it to Lizzie and me in her will, although it was held in trust by my parents. They were renting it out at the moment, but with Lizzie gone, the minute I turned twenty-one it would be mine, along with a small inheritance. Maybe enough to set up a business, if I kept saving in the meantime...

"Not for another four years," Mum snapped, bursting my bubble. "Unless you're planning on getting married before then. God knows you seem determined to do everything except what's best for your future."

"Laura," my dad said to my mum wearily.

"Are you really planning on spending the next four years keeping me prisoner instead of listening to what I actually want?" I asked. "You can't just copy and paste Lizzie's future over mine."

"Don't talk about your sister that way." Mum's voice almost broke and Dad said, "Being overdramatic isn't helping anyone, Megan."

"Overdramatic! Just admit it, you don't trust me to make my own decisions about my own life!"

"Look." Dad sighed, then spoke again, trying to sound reasonable. "I think we all need to step back from this for the evening. We're just upsetting each other. It's Friday night. How about we order a takeaway, watch a movie and pick this up again tomorrow. Then we can have a sensible talk about it all before we speak to the college on Monday morning."

"I'm not sure what there is to talk about." Mum's arms were folded and her elbows stuck out like spikes. "She's seventeen. She's still a minor."

"*She's* sitting right here," I snapped.

"Chinese or Indian?" Dad pulled the menu file from under the coffee table. "Or we could try the new Mexican, if you fancy going out? It's still early…"

"I ate at college," I lied. "And I'm meeting Becca

later, anyway. I need to get ready."

Suddenly, I didn't care about having to be nice to Dylan to get my drinks. I needed a night at the cove, a drink or two (or three) and a chance to shake off all the things I could never be.

I got up from the couch, stretched and headed upstairs to change, my parents' disapproval following me as obviously as the cat padding along behind me. I ignored the feeling, frowning instead at the huge canvas photo of Lizzie at the top of the stairs.

There was something else niggling at the back of my mind. A half-formed memory, or idea, or something.

Something that might be a way out.

Elliott

Sean was waiting for me in the kitchen when I walked in the door.

"You've got post." He was crunching his way through a bowl of cereal – his usual mid-afternoon snack – so the words came out more like 'Oove ot ost'. But then he nodded at the stack of thick envelopes sitting on the edge of the tiny kitchen table and I understood. He swallowed the cereal. "What did you do? Send off for a Russian mail-order bride?"

I dumped my bag in the corner and rolled my eyes. Since every one of those envelopes was emblazoned with a university logo, even Sean wasn't dumb enough not to know what they were.

Prospectuses. That I hadn't sent away for.

Mum was interfering again, then.

"You going to open them?" he pressed, spoon hanging from his fingers and dripping milk on to the wooden tabletop. I glanced at him, surprised. Sean wasn't really the kind of guy to get excited about university prospectuses. He'd barely even leafed through his own last year. Now, if it really had been mail-order bride stuff, he'd have opened them already.

"Gonna take a shower first," I answered, putting off the inevitable conversation about my future. I wasn't going to try and figure it out while I was cold, damp and salty from sea spray, with sand still between my toes.

Sean looked me up and down. "Yeah. Right."

The shower was warmer than the beach by about a dozen degrees but I couldn't focus on the way the water felt. My mind kept getting drawn back to my conversation with Megan that afternoon. She'd *apologized*. I hadn't been sure until today that she even knew how.

I'd wanted to be mad with Megan that morning after Lizzie died. But I'd known that every horrible thing she'd said to me was out of grief, that she was hurting far more than she could ever hurt me.

But now … there was so much I hadn't told her about that night. About Lizzie's frame of mind. About why she'd got drunk and gone out with Evan on the boat.

That was the part that had everyone confused. Even the judge had sounded baffled as he'd heard what a perfect student Lizzie was – an example to the other young people of St Evaline and all that stuff. Why would someone like Lizzie go along with stealing a boat and taking it for a drunken joyride?

Only I knew the answer to that. And I wasn't about to tell anyone.

It wouldn't make a difference now, anyway.

I tried to push thoughts of Lizzie and Megan out of my mind but that just brought me back to thinking about the stack of envelopes on the kitchen table. My alternate futures, in half a tree of paper.

I'd tried to put it off but the UCAS forms needed to be in by mid-January and the tutors at college were already starting to make a fuss about university visits, course requirements and the like.

At some point, I was going to have to break it to them that I wouldn't be applying.

What was the point? University was hardly a guarantee of a job these days, so why should I pay nine grand a year for the privilege? My grades, passing my exams, getting my application in on time … none of that meant a thing if I couldn't find a way to pay for it. In the end, it came down to money.

Dad would have quipped 'doesn't everything?' It sure as hell did for him – so much so that it drove him to embezzlement, fraud and general despicableness.

That was why he was locked up right now, along with the woman he was sleeping with on the side. It was why I was in this mess in the first place.

Mum was already working two jobs just to keep us housed and fed – and work around here was seasonal at best, so right now those jobs didn't have too many hours for her. Sean was at uni studying Engineering on his Navy technical scholarship and spending his summer holidays training with the Navy, so we didn't have his income from weekend work on the fishing boats any more. All the money I got from *my* part-time job already went on household expenses.

None of that added up to three years of expensive and useless education. There wasn't any point even thinking about it. Drying off, I pulled on jeans and a T-shirt and padded barefoot to the kitchen to face the post.

Sean was still sitting there, bowl empty, playing with his spoon. I got the weird feeling that he was waiting for me. I dragged out a chair at the opposite end of the table, wincing at the sound as it scraped a mark along the worn lino, and settled down to work my way through the pile.

Swansea. Cardiff. Aberystwyth. Obviously Mum liked the idea of me being close to home. But there were a few further afield, too. Lancaster. Nottingham. Exeter. Sheffield. Newcastle. Even UCL in London.

I reached for the last envelope only to discover it didn't look quite like the others. I tore it open and read the cover.

A Life Without Limits, the headline yelled, above a photo of three students in Navy uniforms. I looked up; Sean was watching me. Apparently Mum wasn't the only one interfering in my future.

"Just a thought," he said with a shrug. "There are all sorts of bursaries available. You could study something useful. Something you might actually earn a living from."

"You sound like you've been talking to your father." Mum snapped from the doorway, a basket of washing resting on her hip. I winced. 'Dad' was a curse word invoked only rarely in our house, for obvious reasons.

I hadn't visited him since he went away. Hadn't wanted to. He'd only lie to my face, like he had to the rest of the town. I didn't want anything more to do with him. Neither did Sean, as far as I knew. But from the guilty expression on my brother's face, it looked like something had changed.

"I went to see him," he admitted. "We talked."

"What the hell for?" I said. The man ruined our lives. What could possibly make Sean want anything to do with him now?

"He asked me to," Sean said. "He's still our dad."

"Not as far as I'm concerned," I shot back.

It wasn't just the people of St Evaline that he had betrayed. We'd been betrayed, too. He'd been cheating on Mum for years, it turned out. And all the savings she'd put by, all the investments we thought we'd had … that was all gone. Not to mention any dignity we had left.

He'd stolen our futures, our opportunities, our reputations. Just like Dylan thought I'd done to Evan. Difference was, Evan had done something to deserve it.

Mum's face was pale and drawn. "Are you going to go again?" she asked.

"I don't know."

Mum nodded at Sean's reply and put the basket down on top of the prospectuses without looking at what she was doing. Sean grabbed his cereal bowl out of the way just in time.

"What did you talk about?" Mum asked. She sounded so sad, so let down. I could feel the anger seething out of me again – at Dad, and at Sean for letting his influence back into the house.

"Uni. The Navy. He wanted to know how you both were. What Elliott was planning for after A levels."

"I'm amazed he even remembered how old he was," Mum muttered.

"Why does he care?" I asked. He hadn't cared about my future when he lied, cheated, stole and got locked up. Why start now?

"He doesn't." Mum's mouth tightened and she shook her head, a few strands of dark hair tumbling down. "And you don't have to let him be a part of your life. You decide what you want to do and go for it. You're a bright boy, Elliott, everyone has always said so. You could get in anywhere. Study medicine or law or anything! Don't you worry for a moment about what your father thinks."

"I wasn't."

"Good. That's good." Mum flashed me a too-bright smile and grabbed one of the prospectuses that wasn't covered by the laundry. "That's why I sent off for these, love! So you can find your dream. Follow your heart." And all the other Disney clichés, presumably.

She flipped through the UCL prospectus then shoved it under my nose. "Look at this! You can study Archaeology at this one! Remember that time we took you to the British Museum when you were little?"

I nodded slowly. I'd been maybe ten at the time but the memory of the grand hall was burned into my memory. It must have been one of our last trips as a family, before everything went down with Dad.

I remembered every single thing about that day. The way it felt like I'd come home as I walked round those exhibits, staring at mummies and statues and hieroglyphs. Like I'd found something that mattered. I couldn't explain it to Sean or Mum and Dad, but looking at the discoveries those archaeologists had made and the things they'd learned from them… I knew that was what I wanted to do, too.

I took the prospectus from Mum and stared at the photo of the head archaeology professor. I *knew* him. Well, not really. But I recognized him. He'd given the talk on the ancient Egyptians that I'd dragged everyone to that day at the museum. He was the person who'd inspired me. When I was ten, I wanted to be an archaeologist more than anything, to bring my finds home to the British Museum and study them. But since everything had gone to hell I hadn't even let myself think about it. Why admit what I wanted if I couldn't have it?

I slammed the prospectus shut. "I'm not going to university."

"Elliott! Of course you are." Mum shook her head. "You are not going to let That Man stop you getting what you want out of life. I mean it."

"Maybe I just don't want to go," I said. "Did you

think about that? Maybe I'm happy here."

Mum's answering laugh was hollow and I knew that was one lie she'd never believe. But it didn't matter.

I knew my future was right here in St Evaline. There was nowhere else for me to go.

BECCA
Welcome home! You've missed ALL the fun. See you at the cove tonight? Bx

SEAN
Hey. What fun? And might be coving, not sure.

BECCA
Um, you know. The usual fun. That people have around here in winter.

SEAN
So ... no fun at all then?

BECCA
Not much, no.

SEAN
I think you just missed me, because it was boring as hell around here with me out of town.

BECCA
Ego much?

SEAN
So I'm right?

BECCA
Maybe. But the beach should be fun tonight. You really should come.

SEAN
Maybe I'll see you there then.

BECCA
Maybe you will.

Megan

Becca was waiting for me by the railings when I finally escaped my parents. She had her phone in her hand, tapping away at the screen, and didn't even notice I was there until I stood right in front of her.

"Ready?" I asked.

"For the cove? Always." She glanced back down at the screen. "We're a bit early though, aren't we?"

"Got something I need to do first," I explained. "Plus I couldn't stay in that house a minute longer."

"Another argument with your parents?"

"Good guess."

We headed along the pavement that separated the town from the rocks that led down to the beach, Becca shoving her phone in her jeans pocket as she followed me. The night air was bitter and I couldn't wait for a campfire in the cove and a drink to warm me up.

"Where are we going?" Becca asked, matching my stride.

"I need to meet Dylan behind the shops." He'd texted while I was choosing what to wear. Which was funny because I could have sworn he'd said he was going to delete my number after I broke up with him last year.

The original story around school was that he'd got what he wanted and dropped me. The counter story – the one that was closer to the truth and heavily encouraged by Becca – was that he'd been so rubbish in bed that I'd dumped him. That one caught on pretty fast, much to Dylan's annoyance.

The actual truth was so obvious I couldn't see why anyone believed anything else. I'd finished with Dylan because his brother was responsible for Lizzie's death and wouldn't admit it. In Dylan's brain, Evan was still the superhero big brother he'd always been.

After Lizzie, I just wasn't so interested in boys. I didn't want anyone 'getting to know the real me' or asking me how I was feeling. And I was pretty sure they wouldn't like the answers I had to give, anyway.

"Dylan?" Becca groaned. "Don't tell me that's back on again. Do you know how much time and effort I put into convincing people that he was a rubbish shag? Don't make me undo all that."

"It is absolutely not back on," I assured her, shuddering. "Your efforts were not wasted."

"Good. Then why do we have to go meet him?"

"Because he's getting us our drinks." Becca stopped walking but it took me a couple of steps to realize. "What?"

"Have I ever, in the history of our friendship, not got served alcohol when we needed it?" Becca sounded indignant. "What did you need to ask him for? He's not even eighteen."

"It was a diversion tactic." I didn't really want to explain about the scene with Elliott but I wasn't sure how to avoid it now. "He was making trouble down on the beach earlier. I intervened and distracted him by sending him, Freddie and the others off to get the drinks in."

Becca's eyes narrowed. "Making trouble? Trouble for who?" She really never had liked Dylan. She's an excellent judge of character, Becca. I should listen to her more often.

"Elliott," I admitted.

"Elliott Redwood?" Becca's eyebrows shot up. "I thought you two didn't talk any more. After... Well. Everything."

I shrugged and started walking again. "I figured it

was time to move on."

"Really?" Becca scurried to catch up. "And what brought about that sudden change of heart?"

"Well, if you're planning to make shagging Sean a regular occurrence, I figured I'd best be on speaking terms with his brother before the wedding." I flashed her a smile and picked up speed. "Now, come on! Or Dylan'll give my beer away to some fifteen-year-old blonde freezing her tits off in a miniskirt."

Elliott

Sean knocked on my bedroom door twenty minutes after I stormed out of the kitchen then opened it without waiting for an answer. "Mum sent these up." He held up the pile of prospectuses.

"Shove them on the desk." God only knew why she'd bothered. I'd made it pretty clear I wasn't going to look at them.

Sean dumped the prospectuses then leaned back against my desk chair, watching me.

I stretched out on the bed and ignored him, trying to focus on my book instead.

"It's Friday night. You coming out?"

"Where?" I was being purposefully difficult, I knew. But Sean deserved it. "I'm flat broke, so unless your student loan is lasting way longer than expected, we can't afford a night on the town."

"Some people are heading down to the cove tonight,"

Sean said with a shrug. "Thought we might check it out. For old times' sake."

The cove. Amy would be there, along with the usual crowd. I hadn't seen her all day, although we'd made vague plans to catch up tonight. Plus some of the guys were planning on taking their guitars and stuff. It could be fun.

Not to mention the fact that I'd told Megan I'd see her there, or at least let her assume I would be. Given that today was the first time we'd spoken in over a year, I should probably show. But then, what was the point in trying to mend that friendship? We hadn't been close in years, even before Lizzie's death – and I knew some of that had to do with my dad. Megan wouldn't care but her parents would. It wouldn't surprise me if she'd been warned off me, or if her parents had simply made it difficult for us to get together, once we'd moved away from next door. With going up to secondary school and being in different classes … it would have been easy.

And now we were six months from finishing school. Next year Megan would probably go off to uni and I'd only see her in the holidays, if then. She'd have new friends, a new life.

Probably better to just let it go and move on.

Except, she'd asked if she looked like Lizzie and I

couldn't help but think that she might be doing the exact same thing her sister had that last night – trying to be someone she wasn't.

"Come on, El," Sean said, holding out a hand to pull me up. "This might be my last weekend home until Christmas. We should make the most of it."

"Fine. But I have conditions."

"Name them," Sean said, handing me my coat.

"We don't talk about university."

"Done."

"Or Dad." That one was a deal breaker.

Sean paused. "Look, El—"

"I mean it, Sean. I don't want to talk about him. I don't even want to *think* about him. OK?"

Sean sighed. "Fine. No Dad talk tonight."

Or ever. "Great. Then let's go."

Megan

For a Friday night in November the cove was packed.

Becca and I had collected the bottles from Dylan and Freddie, escaping after a few smiles and without making any promises, even when Dylan said he'd see us after, down at the cove. They were off to someone's house first to play computer games or something. I had no doubt by the time they showed up they'd all be drunk but we'd just have to avoid them.

And, like I said, the cove was packed, so it wasn't like there weren't other people to talk to.

Over at the far end, just before the beach hits the cliff wall, someone had started a campfire and there were already a couple of guys with guitars and open cans. Perfect. Just what I needed – a night of fun to take my mind off everything.

The cove in winter was always a bit hit and miss. Some weeks it was dead and Becca and I would shiver for ten minutes or so before giving up and heading home. But some weekends, for no obvious reason, would just be awesome – loads of people, music, fires – a real party. Of course, unless we showed up every week just in case, those wild, one-off weekends often turned out to be the ones Becca and I had opted to stay in with a movie.

Tonight, however, we were there. And we weren't the only ones. I nudged Becca in the ribs. "He came."

Becca looked up and, to anyone except me, it would have seemed like a casual 'don't care' glance. But Becca's my best friend and I know when she's faking it. And right then, she was practically vibrating with nerves, even if no one else could see it.

"Yeah? He said he probably would when I texted." Or, actually, when *I* texted. Still, she'd taken that initial contact and run with it so it was mission accomplished.

We made our way across the sand, towards the fire. I found a relatively dry spot and dragged Becca down to sit beside me. And if our spot conveniently gave Becca the ideal position to watch Sean from, well, I'm just that good a friend.

"What happened with your parents?" Becca asked over the sound of two guitars that weren't quite in tune with each other. "You didn't say before."

I shrugged. "The usual." Becca waited patiently, so I sighed and filled her in on the conversation.

"I think... I think they want me to live the life Lizzie would have lived," I finished. "Like since she's gone, someone has to live up to their expectation of what a perfect daughter should be."

Becca frowned. "I'm sure they don't," she said, but even she didn't sound very convinced and her eyes slid away as she spoke.

I followed Becca's line of sight, watching as Sean opened another can of beer and handed it to Elliott. For a moment, I wondered how I was supposed to act around him, after the scene at the beach earlier. Then I shrugged to myself. He was still just Elliott, after all.

For years, when we were kids, Elliott and I had been inseparable. We'd roamed around the beach together – learning to surf and rock-pooling and exploring the caves in the cliffs. Later, we'd follow Sean down to the cove with his mates, watching to see what life would be like when we were that age. Never mind that Sean was only a couple of years older than us, in the year above Lizzie – when we were eleven, that seemed like an eternity.

But then everything went down with Elliott's dad and there were whispers and rumours all over

St Evaline. They moved across town, and I guess that's when puberty kicked in and we got all awkward around each other. Somehow it was just easier to let our friendship drift. I couldn't remember the last time I'd had a conversation with him before Lizzie died.

Elliott these days ... he wasn't *my* Elliott. He'd grown up into someone entirely different. This Elliott didn't smile so easily, didn't talk so much.

And those weren't the only ways he'd changed. My Elliott had been a scrawny little boy with a fishing net.

This Elliott ... really, really wasn't.

I watched as he lifted a beer can to his mouth, tilting his head back, his dark hair falling away from his forehead and his Adam's apple bobbing as he swallowed. He was wearing a battered old canvas jacket that might have been Sean's but it fitted his broad frame perfectly. I didn't know this new Elliott at all.

Becca was a great best friend. But sometimes I missed that little boy who had been my first friend.

I looked away, back to Becca, who was still staring at Sean while pretending to check her phone. Rolling my eyes, I grabbed the phone from her, opened the camera app and took a few quick, easy shots. "It'll last longer," I told her, as I tossed the phone back into her lap.

Blushing, Becca returned her full attention to me. "So, what did you tell your parents?" she asked.

It was all right for Becca; she knew exactly what she wanted to do, where she needed to study and what grades she needed to get. If you wanted to be a marine biologist it seemed like there was a pretty defined path. Photographers, I figured, probably made it up as they went along.

Luckily, I've always been good at improvisation.

"I told them I'd move to London instead of going to uni," I said.

Becca drew in a breath and stared at me. Becca hates London. "What did they say?"

"That they wouldn't support me. And that I couldn't inherit Grandma Alice's flat to live in for another four years unless I got married..." I trailed off, a possibility flashing in my head like a neon sign.

"Married?" Becca asked, her tone incredulous. "Why on earth would you have to get married?"

"Because those are the terms of Grandma Alice's will," I said slowly, thoughts whirring through my brain. "She left me her flat in London. It's mine the minute I turn twenty-one or when I get married. *Whichever happens first.*"

I stared at Becca and she stared back, her eyes getting

wider and more alarmed by the second. "Hang on. You're not seriously thinking of getting married just to avoid doing a law A level and applying to university?"

"Of course not," I said.

Becca blew out a sigh of relief. "Good. Because—"

"I'm thinking of getting married so I can escape this place and start living my own life." The idea crystallized in my mind and suddenly I knew exactly what I needed to do. Because if the last year of constant battles with my parents had taught me anything, it was that they weren't going to give up their death grip on my future without a fight. Unless I came up with some big guns, and fast, I'd end up living the life they'd imagined for Lizzie for at least the next four years. And then it would be all 'You don't want to waste that expensive education, Megan. Get a proper job. It's time to be a grown-up now'. I knew my parents, I knew how they worked.

And if I had to get married at seventeen to break free, then I would.

Becca scowled at me. "And who exactly are you planning on proposing to?"

I leaned back and settled on to my hands. "I haven't got that far with the planning yet." The guitars were still playing, the fire still burning, everyone was still chatting and drinking as if nothing had changed. But it had. *I* had.

I'd found a way out. And the more I thought about it, the more perfect it seemed. I could move to London the minute I turned eighteen and there was nothing my parents could do about it. Without rent to pay, surely I'd be able to find a good enough job to pay my bills and get started on my career as a photographer.

"I'm pretty sure having someone to actually marry is, you know, the first step in planning a wedding." Becca tucked her feet under her, kneeling up on the sand as she faced me. She was right, I realized. If I found the right person, they could move to London with me and we could split the bills. That would help. The flat even had two bedrooms. It was perfect. "Seriously. What the hell, Meg?"

"Look, I'm still working on it." I sat up straighter to match her. Becca went along with most of my ideas, even when the only justification I could give was 'Death or Glory, Think of the Story'. If she thought this was a crazy idea, maybe I was more doomed than I thought. But it was the only out I could see, so I was sticking with it.

"OK. I get that you want to change your course and stuff," she said slowly. "But don't you think getting *married* is a little extreme? I mean, you're kind of stuck with the other person then, right?"

She wasn't getting it, I could tell. "In a real marriage, yeah, of course. But that's not what this is."

"Then what is it?" Becca asked, the firelight dancing across her skin. "Because I'm totally lost."

I moved closer. "All I really need is a piece of paper saying I'm married and suddenly my life is my own. I won't have to listen to my parents telling me that they get to choose what I do, just because I'm seventeen instead of eighteen." The worst part was, as an August baby, I'd be a minor until the month before I left for university. But if I was already married, they'd have to accept that I was an adult, capable of making my own decisions. I'd get to do what I wanted – even if they wouldn't support me – once I had Grandma Alice's money and the flat waiting for me in London. And they'd have to kick their tenant out, too.

Becca blinked. "OK, that I get. You want to live your life, not Lizzie's."

"Exactly. And they're never going to let me do it while I'm living in their house or while I need their money. So, London."

"And marriage." Becca said the word like it was something holy. Somehow I didn't think we saw the aftermath of a wedding in quite the same way. "Are you even allowed to get married at seventeen?"

"Not without your parents' consent." I grinned. "At least, not in England and Wales." I gave her a minute and she caught on.

"Gretna Green," she whispered. "Seriously?"

We'd both read the same romantic novel back in Year 8, when she'd swiped it from her mum's bookshelf. That story of a young lady whisked off to Gretna Green by a disreputable earl was our first introduction to books with more than kissing in them. "Seriously. You can get married there at sixteen even without your parents agreeing or anything. I looked it up once." Back when I thought I was madly in love with some guy four years older than me who barely noticed I existed. I don't go small with my crushes.

"Wow." Becca sat back. Apparently I'd finally convinced her that I really wanted to do this. "But, wait. Who are you going to marry?"

I gave her a slow smile. "Well, you know, they *did* change the law recently..."

Her eyes went super wide and she started shaking her head from side to side so quickly her black curls whipped around her face. "No. Absolutely not. I am not marrying you."

"Oh, come on! It's not like it would be a real marriage or anything." As far as I was concerned, marriage was just a piece of paper, anyway. I mean, look at my parents. They'd been married for twenty years and I still wasn't sure if they even *liked* each other. They ran the whole thing like an extension of their business dealings. Why shouldn't I use marriage to my advantage in the same way they did?

"Exactly!" Becca yelled, then clapped a hand over her mouth when the group of guys sitting next to us turned to stare. "Exactly," she repeated, quieter this time. "When I get married, I want it to be the real deal. I want the whole package – the dress, the diamond, the big party – and a handsome prince, thank you very much. Much as I love you."

"Fine." I hadn't really thought she would, anyway. But it was worth a shot. "All I actually need is someone who wants to move to London—"

"Which I don't," Becca interjected. "I have plans. And they involve being near the sea."

"I know that. Plus you're scared of the underground." Our only trip to London with my mum had been a disaster. After the first attempt at a tube journey it had mostly involved buses. "Anyway, I just need someone to move to London with me, live in the spare room of the flat and split the bills. Then when my photography business takes off we can get a divorce. Easy."

But Becca was shaking her head again. "Who do we know that is that desperate?"

"Hey! I could have guys lining up to marry me."

"Guys who'd be willing to sleep in your spare room?" Becca raised her eyebrows and I saw what she was getting at. This wasn't a romantic novel. I didn't want someone who expected a real relationship or even a 'friends with benefits' arrangement. I needed an actual friend. "Say you went through with this, do you really think you'd find someone who'd marry you just for your flat?" She made it sound like a joke, a crazy scheme I'd change my mind about in the morning. But it wasn't.

"I need someone I can trust," I said, thinking it through. It was a shame Becca wouldn't do it, because I trusted her more than anyone. "Someone dependable."

"And desperate," Becca repeated. "I don't think there's anyone——"

Over at the fire, there was a burst of laughter and we both looked across automatically. Sean lay flat on his back on the sand, Elliott offering him a hand up.

Sean said something as he brushed the sand from his jeans and Elliott laughed. His voice was deeper and darker than I remembered but somehow the memory of it reverberated through my body all the same.

"Elliott," I whispered. While we might not be the same kids who'd been best friends all those years ago ... I trusted him.

I'd been mad at him after Lizzie because he'd been there and I hadn't − and he hadn't been able to stop her like I would have. But I knew that wasn't his fault. And after his testimony at the trial, I knew he'd done everything he could to help her.

Would he be as willing to help me?

Almost without thinking, I got to my feet. I could go and ask him right now. One fiancé, no waiting. It was perfect.

Becca grabbed my hand and pulled me back down again. "You're not serious! This is a terrible idea."

"Why?" The more I thought about it, the more I realized that Elliott was *perfect*. I'd known him forever and, most importantly, I used to be able to talk him into anything − from spying on Sean and his girlfriend at the beach to stealing sips of his dad's whisky.

"Elliott is..."

"What? Give me one reason why Elliott isn't a good choice that isn't 'he's Sean's brother'."

Becca pulled a face. "You mean besides the way he barely talks to anyone any more and the fact he has a girlfriend?"

I shook my head. "It doesn't matter. It's not like I'm asking him to actually fall in love with me. I don't care if he dates someone else. What else have you got?"

Becca was silent for a long moment. Then finally she said, "But he IS Sean's brother!"

"So? Why should the fact you had a one-night stand with Sean three months ago mean I can't marry Elliott?"

"Do you have any idea how ridiculous that sentence sounds?"

"Not the point." I waved her objection aside. "Look, when we were kids Elliott was always talking about moving to London. Ever since he went to the British Museum. I'd actually be doing him a favour." This could totally work out for both of us.

"Right." Becca didn't sound convinced.

"Well, at least I can offer, right? I mean, there's no way his mum can afford to pay for him to go to uni. He could probably use a free place to live." Everyone knew that Elliott and Sean's mum had been working two jobs ever since their dad was sent to prison.

Becca shook her head. "Do you honestly believe that you're doing this for Elliott now?"

"I'm doing it for me," I replied, bristling at her words. "But if I can help out a friend, why shouldn't I?"

"If he's anything like his brother, he'll leave town the minute you say 'I do'," Becca said.

"As long as he takes me with him, that's fine." But I knew that wasn't what she meant. "Look, let's go over. You can talk to Sean..."

Becca dipped her head so her hair hid her face. "I don't know. I mean, he's leaving again soon. And really, maybe it's better that it was just one night."

"Except you thought it was something more than that," I pointed out. "And it still could be. I mean, come on. We've got the moon, the firelight, the music..." Somewhere over by the fire, a guitar string broke with a loud *twang*. Becca and I exchanged a look and tried not to giggle. "It's super romantic," I finished, grinning.

"Not as romantic as an elopement to Gretna Green," Becca joked.

"Ha! I think this might be the least romantic elopement in history."

"Do you really think you can convince Elliott to go along with it?"

I stood up, brushing the sand from my jeans. "Let's go and find out."

Elliott

Some days, the beach felt more like home than my house did.

That sounds bad. OK, I hate my house, but it's not like I hate living there with my mum and even Sean, most of the time. It's just that they're ... big people. Not physically but in themselves. Their personalities. They talk and yell and live out loud, and that sort of person takes up a lot of the air in a place. And when you have two of them...

I'm not like them. I'd rather lock stuff away than have everyone see it.

Anyway. The beach had air to spare and the waves could even drum out their voices in my head, sometimes.

Normally I preferred the wide-open spaces of the beach, with nothing but sand and sea for miles, when I wanted to escape. But sometimes the cove, a hidden bay just beyond the cliffs, was just what I needed. I had a feeling that tonight might be one of those nights.

I needed to remember why staying in St Evaline was the right choice for me. I needed to focus on all the good things and not think about the life I could have somewhere else.

The cove was rammed but Sean and I managed to weave our way through the crowds to the far side, by the cliffs, where Amy and the guys were waiting for me. Jack and Dewi already had the guitars out and a few people were singing along.

Amy stood up, smiling, as we approached. She brushed the sand from her long red skirt and reached up to kiss me.

"Hey, you," she said as we broke apart. "I was beginning to think you weren't going to make it."

"And miss this kind of musical genius?" I said. "Never."

"You should have texted," Amy added. "I like to know where you are. What you're doing."

"Even if it's 'down at the harbour, cleaning bird muck off a boat'?"

"Even then." Amy's words came out like a command, which gave me an uneasy feeling. There was nothing wrong with her wanting to know where her boyfriend was, I supposed. I just wished it didn't feel like she didn't trust me.

She pulled me down to sit beside her on the sand and Sean rolled his eyes. I'd never got a straight answer from him about why he didn't like Amy, which made me think he didn't have a good reason. Sometimes Sean was like that. He either hated or loved people on sight and nothing would ever shift his opinion.

Well, he was probably going to have to get used to Amy. If I was staying in St Evaline, it figured I'd be staying with her. We'd been together over a year now and things were OK with us.

I took the beer Sean handed me and tried not to examine why the idea of a life with Amy, here at home, didn't make me feel happier.

Sitting back, resting against the cliff wall, I tried to lose myself in the music and the beer, hoping to forget about Sean going to see Dad and the stack of useless prospectuses sitting on my desk at home. It wasn't working. I was starting to think that nothing would when Megan and Becca approached us from the other side of the fire.

"Hello," Sean said, under his breath, when they were still a few metres away. "This looks interesting." Megan voluntarily speaking to me twice in one day? That was more than interesting. It was downright suspicious.

I glanced around the fire, seeking out Amy and finding her deep in conversation with a couple of guys from her English class. Hopefully she was distracted enough not to care that I was talking to my ex-best friend. It wasn't that Amy was the jealous type, exactly, but given my toxic reputation in this town she'd never really had to deal with me talking to other girls much, either.

"You do remember that you slept with her in the summer, right? Becca, I mean." Sometimes Sean didn't remember these things and it made subsequent conversations with girls kind of awkward. And awful.

Sean's my brother and I love him. But sometimes he's an idiot. Not that I'd let anyone else say that.

He waved a beer can at me. "I know, I know. We've texted, actually."

I raised my eyebrows. *That* was a surprise. But I was more intrigued by what Megan wanted. Because I could tell from her expression that she wanted *something*. Even at this distance, her eyes were blazing and her jaw was set. It was the kind of look she used to have when we were kids, right before she tried to convince me to go along with some audaciously terrible plan. Like the time when we were ten and we pretended we were sleeping over at each other's houses and hopped on the train to Cardiff instead. Except we forgot that, living next door to each other, our parents might *notice* if we weren't where we were supposed to be. And the fact that Megan left the train times website open on her mum's tablet.

We got caught before we even reached the next town.

Sometimes I was glad Megan had Becca to go along with her plans these days. And sometimes, just sometimes, I missed being the person she'd flash that smile at and say, "Come on. It'll be *fun*." Like having fun was the only thing that mattered in her world.

Maybe if everything with my dad hadn't happened we'd still be that close. Maybe not. Megan had changed as much as I had over the years – maybe more so since Lizzie died.

But one thing I was sure of – my life had been more fun with Megan in it. And right now, I could do with a little easy fun.

"Hey, Sean." Despite her greeting, Megan sat beside me, leaving Becca to take the space next to Sean. "Elliott," she added, giving me a warm smile.

I didn't trust that smile. She wanted something – and while whatever it was that Megan wanted might be fun for her, I was suddenly remembering that it rarely turned out to be easy. Plus I had a really bad track record at saying no to her when we were kids. Now, all grown up, with curves that drove half the guys at our school crazy, those sparkling eyes and something secret hiding in her grin ... resisting could be impossible.

"Ladies," Sean said, in that way he thinks is suave but isn't. "What's up?"

Megan shrugged, her hair bouncing over her shoulders. "The usual. Thought we'd come and see if things were any more fun over here."

"Things are always more fun when I'm in town." Sean stared at Becca as he said this and we all watched her cheeks turn a rosy red. Poor Becca.

"Actually, El, I was wondering if I could talk to you about something," Megan said, lowering her voice and leaning in. "Fancy a walk?"

I raised my eyebrows. Megan hadn't been this close to me in a long, long time.

"A walk on the freezing beach, away from the warm fire and the beer?"

"I'll make it worth your while," Megan said, half-flirting as she got to her feet. I knew not to take it seriously – from what I saw at college, Megan flirted with everybody and that was as far as it went these days. But since we'd gone from not speaking to apologies to flirting in the space of five hours, I couldn't help but think something very weird was going on.

I took the hand she offered and let her help me up, glancing over to check on Amy as I did so. She was still talking, but as I let go of Megan's hand she looked over and clocked us. I smiled and waved at her, hopefully reassuringly.

I'd never cheat on Amy. I'm not my dad, whatever people believe. But from the look on Amy's face, she didn't seem totally convinced.

For a moment, I thought about telling Megan no, walking over and sitting down beside Amy instead.

The swirling sense of frustration and resentment that overtook me made the decision. Amy was the one person who was supposed to see the real me. If even she didn't trust me, what hope was there?

"Come on, El," Megan called, already a few steps ahead. I looked away from Amy and followed.

I'd only had one beer but I was starting to wonder how much Megan had drunk. She seemed almost manic. Overexcited, perhaps. But about what?

We walked back towards the main beach and for a while there was no sound except the fading guitars and conversation, slowly replaced by the lapping of the waves and the wind in the seagrass. Above us, St Evaline glowed in the light from the street lamps, illuminating the beach just enough that we could see where we were going, without relying on the moonlight glinting off the water.

"So?" I asked eventually, after I'd exhausted the limits of my imagination trying to guess what was on her mind. "What's up?"

Megan stopped walking and turned towards me. I stumbled to a stop, too, a couple of paces away from her.

"I have a proposition for you," Megan said, hands clasped in front of her tightly. "One that can help us both out."

"A proposition?" Why did that sound ominous?

"Yes. We should get married."

Suddenly all of Amy's fears seemed reasonable. I stared at Megan, my brain empty of all thought as I tried to make sense of the words.

She had to be drunk. "I think you might change your mind about that when you sober up. Also, no."

"I haven't been drinking." It was the frustration in her voice that convinced me it wasn't the alcohol talking. "I'm serious."

I don't know what I'd been expecting. Maybe something borderline illegal she needed help with. Or a plan to get Becca and Sean together. Maybe some guy's attention she needed help getting rid of. Or that perhaps she just wanted to talk about how things used to be. About Lizzie, maybe. I'd been waiting over a year for her to ask me what happened that night – not just the account I gave in court, but the details, too. She never had.

I'd even let myself consider, just for a second, that she wanted me.

But never in a million years would I have thought of this.

Marriage? What the hell?

"In that case, why?" It had to be some sort of bet, or something. Was she expecting me to jump at the idea, then she could yell 'Gotcha'? Were Dylan and Freddie hiding out by the cliffs, laughing and listening in? I turned to look but there was no one on this empty stretch of beach except us. "You've got ten seconds to convince me this isn't some stupid prank." Because it had to be. Why else would Megan be proposing marriage to anyone, let alone me?

"You remember my Grandma Alice?" she said in a rush.

I nodded. "She wore those scarves with the bells on."

"And she left me and Lizzie her flat. In London." Megan looked up and caught my eyes. Whatever this was, she really *was* serious. "It's mine the moment I turn twenty-one or when I get married. Whichever happens first."

"You want to move to London," I said, slowly, the logic piecing together in my brain. "Like, for university?" Because of course, that would be fine for Megan. Because things just worked out for girls like her. No worrying about how she'd pay for it – she had a flat there already. The rest would just fall into place.

"Not exactly," she said. "But I want you to come with me."

And that was where the whole thing ran off the track in my mind. "Why me?" We'd barely spoken in years.

Except here she was. Asking me to marry her.

"You always wanted to live in London, remember?" She started walking again, further along the beach towards the harbour. "You wanted to study at one of the universities there and work at the British Museum. It was all you used to talk about." For the first time since she appeared by the fire, she looked a little uncertain. "Unless you've changed your mind?"

"That's not going to happen." She had to know why. Everyone did. Ever since my mum got turned down for a loan by the bank and Cassie the bank teller told basically everyone.

"But it could." Megan was bouncing a little as she walked. It was distracting. "That's what I'm saying. I can make it possible for you."

I was pretty sure this was a fantasy for a lot of guys at school – Megan Hughes leading them off for a secluded night-time walk, promising to make all their dreams come true. God knows what they'd make of what she was offering me, though.

"So, what? We move to London together? And I go to university while you … what, exactly?" It sounded ridiculous, every step of it.

"Set up my photography business," Megan said.

"Ha! I bet your parents love that idea." Mr and Mrs Hughes had always turned their noses up at the sort of arty subjects that Megan liked. Science, law, maths – good. Drama, film, creative writing – bad. Photography would definitely fall into the 'bad' category.

Megan pulled a face. "Which is why we have to get married first."

My brain stalled at the idea. *Married? To Megan? What?* seemed to repeat on a loop.

"Explain it to me again."

Megan sighed and pulled her hair up off her face, tying it in a messy bun as she talked. "OK. Here's the plan. We elope, get married in Gretna Green where I don't need my parents' consent. Stupid August birthday. Anyway, then we're free. No one can tell us who we are or what to do any more."

Free. Away from St Evaline.

But what on earth would I do then? University, archaeology, the British Museum … they'd all been a kid's dream. Like growing up to be an astronaut. Not something that actually happened.

"And with this new-found freedom we…" I trailed off, unable to even picture it.

"Move into my flat in London. You can have the spare

room," she added, letting her hands drop away from her hair. She looked younger without it covering her face. "No rent to pay and we'll split the bills. You can go to university like you always wanted to and I can start my career."

"Your career." In my head, I was already figuring out the logistics. Not that I was going to say yes to what was clearly an insane plan, of course. But still … if I did … if I *could*… The loans would cover tuition and the maintenance loan would give me enough to live on *and* send some home to Mum if I didn't have to pay rent. It could actually work.

If I left St Evaline – and Amy and my family and my *life* – behind.

"I told you. I want to be a photographer," she said, her eyes shining in the lamplight from the road above the beach. "Like, a proper one. I'll start in London but eventually I want to go all over the world taking photos – being a travel photographer…"

I knew it wasn't about my future, my dreams, not really. But now I could see how much Megan had invested in it.

"I thought you wanted to be a vet," I said, remembering an injured kitten she'd rescued and nursed when she was nine.

"When I was a kid, sure." She shrugged. "Doesn't everyone?"

And before the vet thing she'd wanted to be an artist. Then, later, a chef for some reason. Megan had never stuck to one idea for very long; she had a tendency to jump from one dream to another. Was this just another passing fad?

"I only ever wanted to be an archaeologist," I admitted, and it felt like giving up a part of me. A secret. But one she already knew – one she'd remembered.

"Because that's what you're *meant* to be." Leaning forwards, so close that I could see the flecks of other colours in her blue eyes, she smiled at me. "So you'll do it?"

"No. I'm not saying that. I can't..." I couldn't begin to list the reasons why this was a ridiculous idea. "Why now? Why decide this now?"

"If I wait until I'm twenty-one..." She bit her lip, looking uncharacteristically nervous. What was she afraid of, I wondered? "My parents... They've got my future all planned out. Only it's not my future. It's Lizzie's. They want me to do all the things she would have done. I'm not even sure they see me when they look at me. I mean, I look just like her."

"No, you don't." My answer was automatic this time. I couldn't let Megan compare herself to Lizzie, the way Lizzie had compared herself to Megan. "You look like Megan."

She looked up at me, her gaze sceptical. "Same hair, same eyes, same smile…"

I shook my head. "No. Lizzie was…" I tried to see her in my mind, so I could find the right words. But all I could remember was her body, laid out on the beach. "You're sharper. More in focus, somehow." I wanted to say 'more alive', which would be the worst word choice ever.

But she was. Everything about Megan sparkled with life and it made me want to reach out and touch her, to try and share some of that light and energy.

I didn't, though. The kid who'd had a crush on his beautiful best friend was long gone. I had a girlfriend, a life in St Evaline. I had to remember that.

Megan frowned. "They still want me to be her."

"And you want to escape."

Her plan was crazy – they usually were. But they always worked out in the end. And they were fun, most of the time.

But this… This wasn't just messing about. This was serious. And if I said no… I had a horrible feeling she'd find someone else who *would* say yes.

Someone like Dylan Roberts, even.

I couldn't let that happen. I had to stop her – which meant I needed to understand her plan and point out why it wouldn't work. How hard could that be?

"How would it work? I'm not saying yes," I added quickly when she clapped her hands together and let out a little squeak. "But if I did..."

"It's a business deal," Megan explained. "A marriage on paper only. We have separate rooms, separate lives. We're friends with financial benefits only."

So no romance, no sex, no falling in love. That made sense. But I couldn't see any other guy agreeing to it. To marrying her? Sure. To separate bedrooms? Less likely. Not that I was going to agree to it, either, even if it was for different reasons.

Except, suddenly that was all I could think about. The idea of *actually* being Megan's... Oh God, her *husband*. She'd be my *wife*. That was just ... insane. Even the idea of living with her, seeing her every day. And, even though I knew that wasn't what she was suggesting, I couldn't stop my brain from going further, to thinking about touching her, kissing her—

"And then when you finish uni and get a job, we get divorced," she finished, bringing me back down to earth.

"Of course." A short-term business deal, just until we both got what we wanted. It made perfect sense, in a weird way. And maybe that one beer had affected me more than I thought, because I couldn't find the flaw in her logic. It was a ridiculous scheme but I couldn't think of a reason why it wouldn't work. Which meant I needed to buy myself some time. "Let me think about it?"

Megan stopped walking, flashed me a smile, then turned and headed back towards the cove. I watched her move in the moonlight; her jeans tight on her long legs, her oversized sweater hanging over her hips under her jacket. I'd be close to her, every single day.

What about Amy? Hadn't I just been frustrated that she wouldn't trust me – and here I was contemplating marriage to another woman. No, not contemplating. Not really.

"You can have tonight," Megan called back over her shoulder. "Then I'll look for someone else."

"One night isn't long to decide the rest of your life," I pointed out as I lengthened my stride to catch up with her again.

She rolled her eyes. "Don't be melodramatic. It's three years, that's all. Besides, if I gave you as long as you wanted to decide, I'd be twenty-one before you made up your mind. I know you, remember?"

She did, I realized, as we approached the curve in the cliff that hid the cove. We were both different people than we'd been seven years ago, before Dad went to jail, before Lizzie died. But underneath all the grief and the hurt … we were still us. And I was starting to think that 'us' had changed less than I'd thought. I was still the sensible one, toning down her plans, telling her not to try to pet the savage dog she'd befriended on the street, not to jump off that cliff to see if she could fly.

Not to get married at seventeen.

I stared after her, watching her slip into place beside Becca and Sean, joining the conversation without missing a beat, as if she hadn't just turned my whole future on its head. The firelight glinted off her hair and the silvery threads in her jumper.

I looked over to where I'd last seen Amy but she wasn't there. I checked my phone, and found a message.

Gone home. Meet me tomorrow at the Blue Fish? I think we need to talk.

I sighed. Another difficult discussion to think my way out of before tomorrow. Great.

But Amy would get over it, probably. Megan... I wasn't so sure. Insane as her plan was, I couldn't help but consider it – if only because it made me imagine what life could be like outside St Evaline, for the first time in years.

Likes: 43

COMMENTS:

Sean Redwood: Nice pic of the bro and me. Didn't realize we were modelling for you, tho...

Becca Maddox: Megan took it. Apparently she forgot her camera and couldn't go more than a few minutes without taking a photo of something.

Sean Redwood: Way to make a guy feel special. Speaking of, what did young Megan want with my little brother last night? All very mysterious...

Becca Maddox: You'd have to ask her.

Sean Redwood: Does that mean you don't know or you're not telling?

Megan

I was glad I'd shared my drinks with Becca and Sean at the beach when, at stupid o'clock the next morning, my parents knocked on my bedroom door.

Pulling a pillow over my head, I called out a muffled permission for them to come in and heard the rattle of the curtain rail as Dad pulled open the curtains, the same way he used to when I was tiny. Brilliant. More grey morning light. Just what everyone wants on a Saturday when they're supposed to be lying in.

"Megan." My mattress dipped as one of them sat on the edge of the bed. I peeked out from under my pillow to see Mum, her best concerned expression on. "We wanted to talk to you."

I shuffled up in the bed, tugging my pyjama top down over my stomach as I propped up my pillow against the headboard and sank back into it. "Didn't you do enough of that last night?"

"I don't think we really came to any conclusions, do you?" Dad leaned against my desk, across the room, and raised his eyebrows at me. They might not have done but I had. Not that I was telling them that yet.

I sighed. "I guess not." I didn't want to have this conversation. Anyway, as soon as Elliott and I followed through with our plan it would all be obsolete.

As long as Elliott said yes.

He totally had to say yes, right?

"We're concerned that your current college isn't the most encouraging environment for you," Mum said, running a finger along the pattern on my duvet cover.

I blinked. "My college?" That wasn't what I'd been expecting. Especially since my sixth form was the only one in a thirty-mile radius, unless you counted the private school ten miles inland, which took boarders and had a uniform that involved hats.

Surely they couldn't be planning to send me somewhere with hats. Not even Lizzie had wanted to go there.

"Your mum and I thought that a more aspiring peer group might awaken your own ambition." Dad inserted what I assumed was fake excitement into his words.

I stared at him in disbelief. "I have ambition," I said flatly. "You just don't agree that it's the right one."

They both chose to ignore that statement of fact.

"Take your friends, for instance," Mum said. "How many of them want to really make something of themselves?"

Like they'd have a clue what my friends wanted. "Name any two of my friends, Mum."

"Well, there's ... Becca, for a start." The distaste in my mum's tone was clear. Somehow my parents had got the idea that Becca was the troublemaker. It was far easier for my parents to blame my friends than accept that their only living daughter might not be everything they'd always hoped for.

"Becca wants to be a marine biologist," I said, taking pleasure in the surprise on Mum's face. "She's got her whole education and career plan mapped out. Has done for years. Is that ambitious enough for you?"

"What about Elliott, then?" Mum pressed. Of course the only other friend they could remember was the guy who I'd barely spoken to for years. Until yesterday.

"An archaeologist," I replied promptly. "He's going to study at UCL and then intern at the British Museum." Well, as long as he married me, anyway.

"Right," Dad said, looking a little puzzled. "But still, looking at your grades… We really feel you could benefit from an environment that prioritizes learning."

"Like a college." Because wasn't that what they were there for?

"Yes. But maybe one with a better reputation…"

I sat up straight. "You are *not* thinking of sending me to the Woolly Hat Academy."

"Woolten Academy has an excellent—"

"They wear hats!" OK, that probably wasn't the strongest argument against moving me to a private school. "Besides, I'll be sitting my A levels in six months, so what would be the point?"

Mum and Dad exchanged a look – the sort of look that suggested I was missing something fundamental.

"Given your grades," Dad started, but Mum took over before he could phrase it nicely for me.

"We think you should resit this year, at Woolten. Get your grades up to the required standard and apply to Oxbridge next autumn."

Hands down, flat out, no. Not a bloody chance.

"No."

"Megan, we just want you to think about your future. About your potential career," Dad said.

"That's exactly what I am doing." I swung my legs out of bed and reached for last night's jeans and jumper, ignoring the campfire smell. Grabbing some clean underwear from my drawer, I headed for the shower.

"Where do you think you're going?" Mum's voice was full of impatience.

I turned back to face them from the doorway. "I'm going to get showered and dressed, and then I'm going to take my camera down to the beach. There's a gallery in town that might be interested in some of my photos." Maybe. If I could take more of the sort Elodie liked.

"I really think we need to talk about this some more," Dad insisted.

I shook my head. "We really don't. I told you: I'm not going to Woolten. I'm not going to Oxbridge. I'm not going to be a lawyer, or a doctor or whatever it is you want me to be – whatever Lizzie wanted to be. I'm going to be a photographer."

And I would do whatever it took to prove that to them.

Even marry Elliott.

Elliott

The Blue Fish Café was practically empty when I arrived the next morning, except for a familiar dark head bent over a stack of glossy brochures at a corner table. Our table.

Amy hadn't spotted me, so I headed over to the counter first. I needed caffeine for this conversation. And possibly some sort of fried breakfast.

The strange discussion with Megan the night before had been rattling around in my head ever since. I still wasn't a hundred per cent sure that her offer was genuine – Megan was the sort of person who had wild ideas, swore up, down and sideways she was absolutely going to go through with them, then forgot all about them by the following week. Even if she hadn't been drunk when she came up with this one, there was a good chance that she'd change her mind before she got anywhere near a wedding ring.

But if she didn't...

The girl behind the counter handed me my coffee and the ticket for my bacon sandwich, and I was out of delaying tactics. When I turned round, Amy was already looking at me, unsmiling, her hand raised to wave me over to our table.

"Hi." I stood awkwardly beside the table for a moment before she nodded a greeting and I settled into the plastic seat opposite her. "What're you reading?"

Amy held up the brochure – a prospectus for Swansea University. The same one I had on my desk at home.

"So." She put the brochure down on the table and folded her hands on top of it. "Do you have anything you want to say to me?"

What did she expect me to say? *I'm sorry for talking to a friend? I'm sorry you left in a sulk?*

Except I wasn't sorry for either of those things. So I stayed quiet.

"No?" She shook her head. "Honestly, Elliott. I really thought you were different. That you weren't like your father, whatever everyone said—"

"I am nothing like my father." I kept my voice calm, even though I was seething inside. The last thing I wanted was for everyone else in the café to start listening in.

"Really? Then how come you left me alone on the

beach last night while you disappeared off with Megan Hughes?" The betrayal shone out from her face even though I hadn't done anything wrong, just like always.

"Hang on a minute," I snapped. Amy jerked back in surprise. "You weren't alone, you were talking with Noah and Rhys – both male, in case you missed it."

"They're friends!" Amy said, indignant. "What are you implying?"

"Nothing at all," I told her. "Same as you shouldn't have implied anything about me talking to a friend, even if she is a girl."

"Not just any friend though, is she, Elliott?" Amy's tone was knowing. Superior. It made my skin itch. "Everyone knows what Megan Hughes is like. How many boyfriends has she had? And you can bet she slept with every last one of them."

"Don't talk about her like that." Calm was rapidly disappearing as an option. Never mind that Megan had been single since Lizzie died. Never mind that it was no one else's business. In St Evaline, everyone believed they had a right to stick their noses in. To pass judgement.

I'd thought Amy was better than that, though.

"She's my friend, and I won't hear you say that about her."

"Even if it's true?" Amy asked. "And besides, it's

relevant, isn't it? Who would let their boyfriend disappear with a girl like her?"

"Someone who trusted their boyfriend." I pushed my chair back from the table and got to my feet. "Megan was my best friend until I was eleven years old. She needed someone to talk to about her future last night and she picked me. OK?"

"You really just talked?" She looked uncertain now, for the first time.

"Yeah. We really did." I grabbed my coat from the back of the chair. "I've got to go."

Amy shot to her feet. "I'll call you later?"

I shook my head. "Not tonight. I need to think about some things."

I grabbed my wrapped bacon sandwich from the waitress as I strode out into the winter sunlight, the sea breeze stinging my face as I headed across the road to the railings above the beach. I walked along the pavement, just far enough to be sure that I couldn't still be seen from the café. Then I stopped, took a seat on the nearest bench and stared out at the waves while I ate my breakfast.

What was I going to do now?

If Amy didn't trust me to take a walk on the beach with another girl, there was no way we'd manage a long-distance relationship if and when she went away to university, even if it was only an hour or two down the coast. And if she thought as badly of me as the rest of St Evaline … did I even want to be with her?

I'd thought I couldn't go along with Megan's plan because of Amy and because of my mum. Well, and because it was mad. But leaving that aside… If I went to London with Megan, I could send money home to Mum. And if Amy couldn't trust me, what future did we have anyway?

I stood up, tossed the wrapper from my sandwich in the bin and leaned against the railings. Down there on the beach, I saw a familiar figure, camera in hand, taking shots of the waves as they rose and fell.

Megan.

My feet were moving before I even processed the thought, leading me down the stone steps on to the beach, taking me to her.

"Meg?" The wind whipped my words away across the sand. She turned to face me, a small frown line between her eyebrows.

"Elliott." She grinned and snapped a quick shot of me as I approached. Then she lowered her camera and waited for me to get close enough that we could talk properly. "You finished thinking already? That might be a record for you."

"Maybe." I didn't have time for jokes today. "Look, you're serious about this? Getting married, moving to London, everything? You really want to do it?"

She nodded furiously. "More than ever."

I took a breath, gave myself one last moment to opt out of the insanity. And then I dived into the madness head first.

"I'm in," I said, watching the wide, wide grin that spread across her face, so familiar, and so full of the old mischief I remembered. "What do we do first?"

Megan

Elliott was in.

I stared at him across a stack of tarot cards on the Oracle shop counter while Becca shuffled through a file of papers. He was fiddling with the netting of a dreamcatcher, setting the lines of thread straight in the wicker circle and smoothing down the feathers that hung from it. The lines of his brow, his cheekbones, his chin … they were all harder than I remembered. He was all angles and sharp edges and I wanted to photograph him properly, just to capture the shadows on his skin.

I should stop staring. Or maybe I shouldn't.

I mean, he was going to be my husband.

Husband.

I'd never really imagined having one of those before.

When I was a little girl, I might have indulged in some of those wedding dreams – imagining the dress and the flowers and acting out a pretend ceremony. When I was very small, I'd had to play the part of Lizzie's bridesmaid until she got too old for games like that and I got to be the bride. But that dream was all about the wedding – the guy playing the husband was the least important part of it all.

Funnily enough, that guy had usually been Elliott.

"So, when do we do this?" I was eager for action. The sooner we got it sorted, the less time Elliott had to back out. I had no idea what had convinced him to make such a monumental decision in record time, let alone decide the way I wanted him to, but I wasn't going to risk whatever it was wearing off. The Elliott I remembered would have had a lot more questions. This one seemed more ... desperate.

"Soon," Elliott said. I glanced at him in surprise. He was definitely under the influence of something.

"Next week?" I suggested.

"Works for me," Elliott said.

"Try next month," Becca said, handing me the papers.

"Why?" I leafed through a few pages, but it was all dense type, so I didn't bother actually reading it before passing them over to Elliott. He could fill me in once he'd scanned through them.

"We have to give twenty-nine working days' notice?" Elliott looked up from the papers, his eyebrows raised. "That's cutting it fine."

"Fine for what?" I asked, frowning.

"UCAS applications," Elliott explained. "If I want to go to uni, mine needs to be in by mid-January, and I want to know this is a sure thing before I apply. No offence Meg, but I can't risk you changing your mind."

"Offence taken," I said mildly. Here I was worrying he was going to back out, only to find he was thinking exactly the same thing. Maybe we were a match, after all.

One thing was certain – Elliott wanted this as much as I did. Needed, even. From what little he'd said, marrying me might be his only shot at going to university. And that was good. The more desperate he was, the more likely it was to work.

"Twenty-nine days … if we get the application in this week, that puts us at what? Christmas?" I asked.

Becca fished her phone from her pocket and tapped on her calendar app. "Just before. But the website says that holidays tend to book up fast. You might have to wait until January…"

Elliott groaned. "Like I said. Cutting it fine."

"Isn't there a way we can do it faster?" I don't like

waiting. And really, the human race had speeded up everything else – communication, travel, photography. How hard could marriage be? "In the book they just showed up and got married."

"What book?" Elliott asked. "Wait, you got this crazy idea from a book?"

"You said yes to this crazy idea," I pointed out.

"I had reasons," Elliott answered.

"It was one of my mum's romances," Becca filled in.

I shot her a glare but she either didn't see it or ignored it. It's hard to tell with Becca sometimes. "We read it years ago. And apparently they've changed the rules since 1876 or whenever it was set."

"So we have to wait a month." Elliott dropped the dreamcatcher to the counter. "Great."

"Actually, it could be a good thing." Becca had clearly embraced the dual role of wedding coordinator and cheerleader. Which, given that I knew she thought the whole plan was insane, said quite a lot about our friendship. Of course, it didn't mean she wouldn't spend the next twenty-nine days trying to talk me out of it. Possibly she was just trying to bore me with details until I gave up on the whole idea.

"Good how?" I asked.

"Well, it gives you two time to hammer out the terms

of your marriage agreement," Becca said, pushing some more papers towards Elliott. "I took the liberty of printing out some sample prenups."

"I don't think either of us is intending to try and get custody of the pet tiger," Elliott said dryly. "Where did you get these from?"

Becca shrugged. "Some celebrity wedding site. I was getting ideas."

"Hang on. We don't need ideas. This isn't a real wedding." Elliott looked across at me for support and I echoed Becca's shrug.

"I tend to leave the details of my plans to Becca these days. She's loads better at it."

"And it *is* a real wedding," Becca said. "At least, in the sense that you need all the usual things for a wedding. A venue, a registrar, forms, a dress, rings…"

I glanced across at Elliott, wondering if he was remembering the same things I was – me draped in a lace tablecloth, him in his jeans, holding a plastic ring with a gaudy glitter bubble on the top.

Probably not.

"Elliott's right," I said, suddenly uncomfortable at the level of detail this plan needed – not to mention the way Elliott was looking at me. Like putting his faith in me might be the worst idea he ever had.

"This is a business deal, not a romance. We don't need jewellery."

"Actually, the ceremony does." Becca shoved an order of service under my nose. And there it was in black and white, with a tasteful flourish underneath. *The exchange of rings.*

"Fine. We'll pick up some cheap ones nearer the time. Let's get back to the stuff that matters. How do we get this thing booked?"

Elliott nodded his agreement. "For as soon as possible. If we're going to do this—"

"We are."

"Then let's get it done." Elliott sounded … resigned. I frowned. Here I was, giving him the opportunity to chase his dreams, and I got the feeling he still thought he was doing *me* a favour.

Which I suppose he was.

Becca sighed. "OK. First, there are forms. Let me get my laptop."

She disappeared into the back room, leaving me and Elliott staring at each other across the counter. For the first time since we'd become friends at the age of about two and a half, I had absolutely nothing to say to him.

All I could think was, *I'm going to marry you.*

Was that exciting, terrifying, or both?

Probably both.

"Right." Becca appeared through the curtain, laptop in hand, and I jerked back from the counter, snapping my gaze away from Elliott's. "Here we go."

We'd almost finished completing the application form when the shop door opened, the tinkling bells chiming in a crazy rhythm. We all looked up in surprise. Nobody *ever* shopped at Oracle except tourists and there were none of them around in November.

"What are you three up to?" Sean leaned against the door as it shut behind him, his arms crossed over his chest and his eyebrows raised. "I saw you through the window. Whatever you're working on looks far too interesting to be homework."

Becca casually shifted the laptop so the screen was facing away from Sean. "University applications. So, not interesting so much as essential."

"I thought that not everyone needed to go to university," Sean said, but he was looking at Elliott. "Apparently there are other options."

"And it's good to keep your options open," Elliott said mildly. "Cover all the bases and so on."

"Yeah? You're applying, then?" Sean asked.

Elliott glanced away and Becca answered before he could.

"I am. To the five universities with the best reputation for marine biology in the country," she said. "Well, the top five by the sea."

"Right." Sean's gaze flicked from his brother to Becca. "I get that. It's good to aim high."

"If you can afford it," Elliott muttered under his breath, but Sean wasn't listening any more. He was staring at Becca.

Interesting.

"Anyway, we're kind of in the middle of things…" Becca trailed off, waiting for Sean to get the hint. Which, unusually for Sean, he did.

"Right." He pushed away from the doorframe and reached for the handle. "See you at home, El."

"Yeah." Elliott sounded thrilled at the prospect.

We sat in silence as the door closed behind Sean and watched him disappearing down the street towards the station end of town.

"He didn't buy it," Elliott said eventually. "He knows I wasn't planning on going to university."

"Doesn't matter," I told him. "We'll come up with an explanation and you'll sell it to him. It's not like he's going to guess what's actually going on, is it?"

Becca giggled and slapped her hand over her mouth. She's always hated her laugh. Says it's too bubbly blonde for her colouring. "Yeah," she said, moving her hand away again. "On Sean's list of things we might be doing, planning an elopement to Gretna Green probably isn't at the top. Or on there at all."

"God, what do you think he thinks we *are* doing?" I couldn't help laughing, either.

"Nothing he would do," Elliott said, sounding far less amused by the idea than we were. I shared a glance with Becca and we both sobered up.

"We're going to need a cover story." Sean's interruption had proved that much at least. We needed a reason to be spending time together and, more importantly, an excuse for why we needed to disappear for a couple of days in January.

"Yeah," Elliott agreed. "Especially since we can't exactly just bugger off to Gretna for the afternoon. It's, what, four hours away? More?" He looked over at Becca for confirmation.

"Six hours if you drive," Becca answered. "Which I suggest you do because the trains are awful. It takes nearly twice as long and costs a fortune."

"We'll have to borrow a car." I looked meaningfully at Elliott, hoping he'd interpret that as '*you'll* have to borrow a car', since I still hadn't passed my test.

"Sean might lend me his," Elliott said, sounding

dubious. "If he's around, anyway. I'll ask. Nearer the time."

I made a mental note to nag him about it regularly between now and then.

"What are you going to tell your parents?" Becca asked.

Elliott and I exchanged glances and shrugs. "History field trip?" I suggested. It was the one subject we had in common.

"Hiking in the Brecons," Elliott countered. "Some sort of extra-curricular thing. It's close, so they won't worry, and has the potential for us to get lost or stranded or something in case anything goes wrong."

I shrugged. "Works for me."

"I can print up some fake permission slips and things," Becca said. "Make it look official. But Elliott … what are you going to tell Amy?"

What did it say about me that I'd almost completely forgotten about Elliott's girlfriend? In my defence, it wasn't like I was *actually* stealing her boyfriend. Just borrowing him, temporarily.

Elliott shrugged. "I'll think of something. And in the meantime… I guess we'll just keep it our secret, yeah?"

I nodded. "Sounds like a plan."

"Great." Was that a hint of anxiety in his tone?

"So all we need to do is get the application in and wait to get confirmation of the date."

We'd chosen the fifth of January as the first post-New Year date after we were back at college. Suddenly, it seemed an awfully long way off.

"Waiting," I said. "My favourite."

Elliott was fiddling with the dreamcatcher again, looking like he might snap the strings he was so tense, and we still had over a month to go. I'd need to keep him close over the next few weeks, I decided. As certain as he said he was, I really didn't want him losing it or changing his mind at the last moment.

Or confessing all to his girlfriend, for that matter. The fewer people who knew about our plans, the better.

It would be our secret.

SEAN
So, what were you guys really looking at this afternoon? *No one* looks that excited about university applications.

BECCA
What else would we have to talk about? We've only got a month and a bit to get them in.

SEAN
Yeah, I'm still not buying it. No worries. I'll just have to get the truth out of Elliott.

BECCA
Good luck with that.

SEAN
You don't think I can do it?

BECCA
I think Elliott will tell you we were filling in UCAS forms.

SEAN
A non-denial denial. Suspicious.

BECCA
Or the truth.

SEAN
Nope. Not buying it. Reckon you might be more likely to tell me what's going on if we went out for drinks?

BECCA
Depends. Is your sudden interest in your brother's life an excuse to ask me out?

SEAN
Maybe.

BECCA
Then maybe.

Elliott

I spent the next week trying to act normal. Which, for me, meant getting on with my own life, ignoring anyone who didn't like me – which was most people – and trying not to show that inside all my nerves were jangling.

Sean went back to university, taking his car with him, so Megan couldn't nag me too much about asking him to borrow it. Not that we were spending a lot of time chatting. We didn't usually and that sort of activity might make people pay attention.

Generally, not drawing attention to myself works out for the best. And Megan *always* draws attention.

Amy, of course, had already paid attention to my sudden reconnection with Megan. And I had no idea what I was going to do about that.

She'd texted me the next day, almost as if nothing had happened. I figured that meant she knew she was in the wrong, which just made me feel a million times guiltier about everything. I knew that if Megan and I went through with our plan, I'd have to tell Amy before then – if we stayed together.

For now, I decided that pretending nothing had happened, and nothing was happening, might be the easiest option.

We went back to college on Monday and, as planned, nothing seemed any different. Except inside me, where I kept the knowledge that I might just have changed my life.

I was engaged. To Megan Hughes. As in, actually getting married, not the sort of 'engaged' that some couples at college were, with a cheapo ring and a vague intention to do something about it one day. We were going through with it.

And no one could even know.

So, for over a week, I barely saw Megan. Amy and I were practically back to normal; Megan still sat in the canteen or the common room with the popular kids and I stayed in the far corner with my friends.

Until the following Monday, when Megan suddenly pulled up an extra chair beside our table in the common room.

"Hey," she said, smiling around the group. They mostly blinked back at her in confusion. I gave thanks that Amy was off at her English class.

Megan waited until everyone had turned back to what they were doing, then reached down into her bag – which meant leaning in closer to me, too. "Becca got the confirmation email," she whispered. "We're on for the fifth of January."

Something ran through my body, making my pulse throb faster. I wasn't sure if it was panic or excitement or some weird mixture of both. Over the last week, I'd been lying awake at night, daring to imagine what it might mean for me and trying to stop myself from hoping at the same time. Could this be my chance to have the future I'd basically given up on, until now?

"So, what's next?" I whispered back, glancing around to make sure no one was listening in. Then, just in case, I motioned Megan over to a couple of spare chairs at the next table. Better safe than sorry.

"We need to pay a deposit for the venue and the registrar and everything." Megan pulled a sheet of paper out of her bag and showed me a printout of a budget.

"Do you think Becca might be getting a little carried away with this?" I asked as I studied the spreadsheet, mentally comparing the amounts to the dwindling sum in my savings account. Mum's car had needed new brake pads that month, plus there was my UCAS application fee to pay…

"I think she's trying to bury me with details." Meg plucked the budget from my hand and shoved it, crumpled, back into her bag. "Like, if she makes it all boring and real I'll decide it's not fun any more."

"Except you're not doing it for fun." If this was all some big prank to her, my future was even more screwed than before.

"No. I'm not." I looked up and saw that her expression was more serious than ever. Whatever happened, Megan intended to go through with this.

I was pretty sure that should be reassuring.

"How much do you need from me?" I asked, trying not to wince as I remembered the total at the bottom of Becca's budget.

Megan waved a hand. "Don't worry about it. This is my crazy idea, I'll fund it."

Part of me felt awkward at the idea of Megan paying for our fake wedding but a larger part was swamped with relief. "You got a secret trust fund I don't know about?" It wouldn't surprise me. Megan's family had never been exactly hard up. They were as well off as we'd been, before Dad left.

"Not until I turn twenty-one. Or get married." She flashed me a smile and a strange warmth filled me up. I hadn't realized how much I'd missed having secrets with Megan. How much I'd missed her as my best friend, the last six years.

But we were all grown up now – and both our futures were riding on us getting married. Which was why, whatever happened with me and Amy, any weird feelings about Megan were getting pitched into the deep hole in my brain marked 'Do Not Think About This'.

"In the meantime," Megan went on, "I have the next best thing. A job."

"A job. You went and got a job, just like that? Where? Doing what?" Part-time jobs were like gold dust around our town in the winter. How the hell had Megan scored one in eight days flat, just when she needed it? Who was that lucky?

"Doesn't matter," Megan said, with a dismissive wave of her hand that instantly made me suspicious.

"It kind of does, Meg," I said, thinking of the printout again. "I mean, I don't want you doing anything dodgy, just to pay for this… I can help out somehow."

"You need your money for other stuff. Don't pretend you don't." She cast me a stern look that was utterly out of place on her face. "Anyway, it's not dodgy. Promise. And it even uses my photography skills."

I think she meant that to reassure me but if anything it only made me more suspicious. But Megan refused to discuss it any further and, leaping up, threw her bag on her shoulder and wandered off again.

"What was that about?" Dewi asked, eyebrows raised, when I rejoined the group.

"History project." The lie came out easily.

"Right. Bet Amy's thrilled about that one." Dewi grinned to show he was joking and I tried to smile back.

"It'll be over soon." That much was true, anyway.

Tugging my ancient phone from my pocket, I texted Becca to see if she had any idea what Megan's new job was.

Her reply came halfway through my next class.

Meet me at the shopping centre on Saturday at 4 and I'll show you.

Megan

The important thing, I reminded myself as I walked through the automatic doors of the shopping centre too early on Saturday morning, was the money. Doing this job would pay for Elliott and me to get to Gretna Green, get married and start our lives in London. I'd be going after the future *I* wanted – not living in my sister's shadow.

And it might not be a dream job but it would be worth it in the end. It wasn't like it was a dream wedding, either. I only had to stick it out long enough to earn the sum at the bottom of Becca's budget.

How hard could that be?

Seven hours later, I was rethinking that assumption.

"I want a new iPad, an iPhone – the newest one, not the old one, I've already got one of those. And I want—"

"I think that's probably enough for my elves to be

getting on with," the world's most patient Santa said, patting the head of the spoilt brat on his knee. "We want to make sure they've got time to make toys for all the other boys and girls now, don't we?"

The little girl looked up at him scornfully. "Elves don't *make* iPads," she said. "Apple does."

"Right." Even Santa looked like he might be about to run out of jolly with this one. "Well, if you look up and smile, my helpful elf will take our photo! Won't that be nice?"

The girl looked me up and down, taking me in – from the jingly bells on the top of my green felt hat, the oh-so-flattering elf costume, complete with crimson ruffles, right down to the bells on the end of my pointy shoes.

If anyone I knew saw me right now, I might have to claim some sort of head-injury-induced amnesia and pretend I thought my name was Glinda.

"Smile," I said, trying to do the same as I raised my camera to frame the shot.

Beside me, the brat's dad elbowed his way in, knocking my shot and ruining the exposure with the flash from his phone as he took a series of snaps in quick succession.

"No point paying over the odds for an elf photo when we can take our own, eh?" he said, nudging me in my green-felted ribs. "Who needs a photographer these days, anyway?"

My face felt as red as the ruffles around my neck and I barely resisted the urge to throttle the idiot with my camera strap.

Santa must have noticed my distress because, in seconds, the brat was off his knee, back in the loving, cheapskate arms of her family, and he was signalling the welcome elf to close the queue.

"Sorry, kids, Santa has to take a little break now," he called out. "But I'll be back in a couple of minutes. And in the meantime, my dancing elves have got a show for you!"

Right on cue, five elves in skimpier green costumes than mine shimmied out from behind the grotto, ready to dance their way through a medley of popular Christmas songs, while Santa downed another cup of coffee and consumed a mince pie in peace.

"Go on, you take a break, too," Santa said, as we moved out of eyesight of the kids. "Elf Kevin can take over with the camera for twenty minutes."

Normally I might have objected, since photos were my job and Kevin was a barely adequate Welcome Elf. But under the circumstances...

"Thanks, Santa."

I darted off towards the staff room, praying that I didn't see anyone I knew between the grotto and the safety of the 'Staff Only' sign. I almost, almost made it, too.

"That's a new look for you."

I paused, hand on the door, and sighed at the amusement in Elliott's voice. Of course. He couldn't just let me pay for stuff, could he? He had to know *how*.

"Becca told you?"

"Becca brought him," Becca said from behind me, and I turned round to make sure she hadn't also brought the entire college, just for a laugh. I jingled as I moved and when I saw them, they were both smirking.

"For the love of God, why?" I asked. "Can't a girl humiliate herself in private these days?"

"We're not here to laugh at you, Meg," Becca said.

"Well..." Elliott added unhelpfully. Becca glared at him. "Right, no, we're not. We're here because...?"

Becca rolled her eyes. "Because you wanted to see how she was earning the money to pay for this crazy plan. Besides, as much as you like pretending that this isn't a real wedding, Megan, I do need to buy *some* supplies before the big day. And this is a shopping centre, so, here we all are. Two birds, one stone, as my dad would say."

I narrowed my eyes at her. "What, exactly, do we need to buy?" It was probably on the budget but I hadn't looked too closely at the detail. I was too busy dealing with the bottom line.

Becca ticked the items off on her fingers. "Rings, a wedding dress – don't look like that, Meg, you've got to wear something! I'm not talking some big meringue thing but if you want the people in Gretna Green to take this wedding seriously and not call your parents, it needs to look like the real deal."

I sighed. She had a point. Even if it was *legal* for me to get married without my parents' consent in Scotland, that didn't mean there wouldn't be some do-gooder there to try to stop us.

"Fine," I said, looking to Elliott for his nod of agreement, too. "But I don't finish work until five, so it'll have to be after that."

Becca smiled the smug smile of the person who has been proved right. "That's fine; shops are open until eight tonight. And anyway, I'm meeting someone for coffee first. I'll see you back at the grotto at five."

"Who are you meeting?" I asked, because that seemed like the sort of thing a best friend should know about.

"Oh, just a friend," Becca said vaguely. But she glanced across at Elliott as she said it, so I knew it was Sean. She checked her watch. "Actually, I'd better go. See you both later!"

"Both?" Elliott asked, as she dashed off towards the escalators. "Does that mean I have to come shopping, too?" He sounded faintly alarmed at the prospect.

"Absolutely not. Don't you know it's bad luck for the groom to see the dress before the big day?" And fake wedding or not, I wasn't running the risk of any bad luck. "But if you do end up hanging around, we could grab dinner later and travel back together?"

"Sounds good," Elliott said, and I felt strangely relieved.

We hadn't actually spent much time together since we'd decided to elope. Here, away from the curious eyes of our friends at college – and his girlfriend – was perfect. After all, we'd be living together in London. We had to learn how to be friends again for that to work.

Elliott and I walked slowly back towards the grotto. I wasn't all that keen to get back to my elf duties and now it didn't seem to matter who saw me.

"So, this job…" Elliott asked, as the grotto came into sight.

"It's just a job," I said quickly. "A short-term gig to get us what we need. Besides, it is, by its very definition, done by Christmas."

"But you're OK with it?" He looked over at me, his forehead crumpled with concern. "I mean, if you hate it, we could always call things off—"

"No. Absolutely not. We are doing this. I can't believe you'd think otherwise."

Elliott sighed. "I didn't, really. But we could find another way to get the money. Probably."

"How, exactly?" Elliott was sweet to worry – I hadn't expected it. I'd figured he'd just let me get on with things then pitch up on the day to say 'I do'. But it seemed like he cared about this, too.

"Honestly, it's fine. I mean, I'm not thinking about switching career paths to become a professional elf or anything, but for now it's fine. Great, even." If you ignored the kids. And the humiliation. "Don't worry. I've got this sorted."

He gave me another searching look, his eyes dark and weirdly compelling. I felt like if I was lying, he'd see it, so I concentrated on looking truthful. "If you're certain," he said.

"I am." Over at the grotto, the dancing elves were curtsying. "And I have to get back to it. So, dinner later? Meet back here at six thirty?"

He nodded and I grinned. It was kind of nice, having Elliott as a friend again. And the idea of having him with me as I started my new life in London ... it was reassuring. Well, mostly. This Elliott wasn't the familiar, comfortable presence I remembered from my childhood. He was something new – intense, unreadable. And the odd feelings that fluttered through me when he looked at me were confusing. And not comfortable at all.

Elliott didn't need to know about those feelings though, I decided, as I hopped over the candy cane rail back into the grotto to retrieve my camera from Kevin. I didn't want to give him any reason to think that our fake wedding was a bad idea.

Elliott

While Megan went back to work, I decided to get out of the shopping centre and go somewhere I could distract myself from the thought that, in an hour or so, she would be buying her wedding dress. For our wedding. A wedding with me in it.

Two weeks on and it was still incredibly weird. I had a suspicion it might be bizarre long past January fifth, too.

Seeing Megan in her elf outfit had made one thing very clear to me – she was going to go through with this.

Which meant I had to get serious, too.

Part of me had assumed this whole thing would fall through before the wedding day. That there was no way we could really pull this off. That's why I'd been delaying filling in my UCAS application and avoiding coming to any sort of decision about what to tell Amy.

But now this was really happening. And I couldn't put those things off any longer.

Outside the wind blew chilly and I wrapped my coat tighter around my body as I headed down a side street. I was halfway to where I vaguely remembered there being a comic-book store when I spotted the second-hand shop.

I'm not normally the sort of guy who browses second-hand shops looking for bargains. I mean, most of our furniture at home either came from or belonged in a second-hand shop. I didn't need to go looking for more. But the window of this shop was filled with jewellery – including a tray of rings. And given the conversation I'd had earlier with Megan and Becca, they caught my attention.

I didn't have much of an idea about wedding rings or what sort of jewellery Meg even liked but I figured it didn't really matter. She'd probably take it off the minute we left Gretna. But if we needed a ring, something in me just couldn't let her buy it for herself. Not even with her hard-earned elf money. And buying a ring – that was definitely taking things seriously. I pushed open the door and stepped in, steeling myself for a conversation with the middle-aged shop assistant in which I'd probably have to lie through my teeth. I mean, what was I supposed to say? 'I'm buying a ring for my fake fiancée so we can elope to Greta to inherit a flat'? She'd think I was crazy. But crazy might be better than 'I'm buying the ring I want the woman I love to wear for the rest of her life from a charity shop'.

Maybe I just wouldn't tell her anything. What business of hers was it *why* I wanted the ring, anyway?

That attitude got me through asking to see the tray of rings in the window, at least. But then the assistant asked, "What ring size are you looking for?" as she placed the tray on the glass counter and I realized I hadn't a clue.

"Um, I'm not sure of the exact size..." I looked down at her hands and mine. Neither of them looked anything like Megan's. "She's got quite slim fingers, though."

The woman looked understanding, at least. "You know, I used to work in a jewellery shop when I was younger and you'd be surprised how many men would come in – lots older than you – to buy jewellery for women they'd been married to for years, or even ridiculously expensive engagement rings, without the first idea what size or style they were looking for!"

I smiled along with her laugh, as if it were ridiculous, unlike my own situation.

"Who are you buying this one for, anyway?" she asked, apparently unable to hold back her curiosity any longer.

"My sister," I lied. "She, uh, she's having a bit of a hard time at school. I thought a surprise might cheer her up."

"Well, you know, we've got some very nice necklaces, too..." She reached behind her to bring out a display board but I shook my head.

"No, it has to be a ring. She, uh, already has a necklace she wears all the time." I sucked at lying. Why was I even bothering? As if this woman cared about Megan and me eloping. But it was our secret – mine, Meg's and Becca's.

"I like this one," I said pointing to the ring that had first caught my eye in the window. It was silver, with sparkly stones that almost certainly weren't diamonds set into the band all the way around. I thought it looked enough like a wedding ring to suit our purpose and had the added benefit of a bit of sparkle.

The lady pulled the ring out of the tray and handed it to me. On a whim, I tried it on my little finger – it fitted perfectly. I reckoned that had to be close enough to the size of Megan's ring finger.

"How much?" I asked, and the lady held the tray up over her head to check the prices underneath.

"Fifteen pounds for that one."

"I'll take it." I pulled out my wallet, thankful for the crazy writer from London who'd wanted an exclusive boat tour of the smugglers' caves last weekend, despite the winter chill.

She slipped the ring into a paper bag and handed it

to me as I gave her the money. But before I could turn around, I heard the door open again. I checked the mirror behind the counter, suddenly nervous. Long dark hair, gorgeous pink lips and a very familiar green velvet coat.

Amy.

What was she doing here?

Her appearing at the worst possible moment seemed like a sign – I couldn't put off deciding what to do about us any longer. It wasn't fair to her and it made me feel awful.

"Thanks," I mumbled to the woman behind the counter, shoving the ring into my pocket as I turned away. For a moment I thought Amy might not have spotted me, she looked so engrossed in the bookshelves. But then she looked up just as I approached and smiled.

"Elliott!"

"Amy. Hey." Even now I wasn't sure what I was going to do. Tell her the truth and hope she'd support me, or break things off.

Neither seemed particularly appealing.

"You didn't tell me you were coming to town today." Amy's smile was friendly but somehow her words sounded possessive. And in the end, that was what made my decision for me. Amy would never trust me in London with Megan. "Um, I'm having dinner with some friends over at the shopping centre later. I thought I'd have a poke around here first."

"Friends?" Amy asked, too casually. "Megan Hughes?"

"And Becca," I added quickly, in case she got the wrong idea. "And possibly Sean actually, I think." Becca might think she was being stealthy about her flirtation with my brother but I'd known Sean too long not to notice when he was playing that interested-not-interested game with a girl. Especially since he'd shown up this weekend, unannounced, just to 'see the family' then disappeared out and ignored Mum and me ever since.

"Sounds like a double date," Amy joked, without any humour in her voice.

"No. It's not like that. I wouldn't... Look. It's just friends having dinner." I sighed. "But Amy... I think we need to talk."

"Yeah." Amy's shoulders drooped. "So... Are you walking over there now?"

I checked my watch. "I guess so. But I have a little time. We could grab a drink first."

"And talk." Amy pushed the book she'd been looking at back on to the shelf, and turned to me with a sad smile. "Great."

We walked in silence back towards the shopping centre, its façade illuminated by Christmas lights. I was pretty sure Amy was waiting for me to say something but I couldn't find the words. The ring felt heavy in my pocket.

This thing with Megan wasn't even real. So why did I feel like my dad, all of a sudden? We stopped at the first coffee shop we came to, on the edge of the shopping centre, and I queued to buy our drinks, running through how I should say it – how to explain everything that was happening. But by the time I placed the tray on the table, I had nothing.

There was no good way to do this.

I'd tried, over the last couple of weeks, to imagine my life without Amy. And weirdly, it hadn't felt all that different. I cared about her and I'd miss having her to talk to. But the more I thought about it, the more I realized that it had been months since we'd had a real conversation – one that mattered. And I wasn't sure why. What had changed?

Amy reached for her mug and looked up at me. "OK, let's not drag this out. I know what's going on here."

For a fleeting moment, I thought she knew about the elopement and my heart jumped up into my throat. "How do you mean?"

"This isn't working any more, is it?" she said plainly, and my heart rate started to slow to normal again.

"No."

"And I think I know why," Amy said. I braced myself for a rant about Megan but then she carried on, "It's the university thing, isn't it? You're mad that I'm going and you're not."

"I'm not—" I started, then stopped. What was I going to say? That actually, I was applying to study in London?

I hadn't even dared to think what might happen if I didn't get in. There were enough universities in the capital that I was hedging my bets, planning to apply to all of them and hoping my marks carried me through. Otherwise... Well, I guess it was back to Plan A and Megan would be going to London alone.

"It's OK," Amy said. "I get it. I'm moving on and you're staying in St Evaline and that's hard. And I realized the other day that I'd been avoiding talking about it, because I didn't want to upset you."

"You shouldn't have to do that." I felt ashamed at the very idea. Here I was, planning my own escape and Amy didn't even feel she could talk to me about hers.

"That's not the worst of it." Amy shook her head. "I realized I was only looking at universities nearby or with good rail links so you could visit. And then the other week, when you went off with Megan ... it brought it home to me that I shouldn't be basing my whole future around who I'm dating at seventeen."

"Yeah, you shouldn't." I sighed. "I'm sorry. I've been crap at this."

"Pretty much," Amy agreed. "But so have I. I mean, we hadn't even talked about what would happen when I went away. I just assumed."

"I think… I think you need to go wherever you want to go, do whatever you want to do and not think about me at all." It sounded selfless but I knew I was only really making my own life easier.

"I think I do, too. Seventeen is too young to be making life choices for someone else." Amy gave me a small smile. "So … that's it for us?"

"Yeah. I guess it is." My chest ached at the idea but I knew it was the right decision. Amy deserved a lot better than I was willing to give her. And I needed to be free to figure out my own future, too.

"And… There's really nothing going on with you and Megan?"

Nothing going on? Oh, there was plenty going on. Just not the way Amy meant.

"We're just friends," I assured her.

"Right." She didn't look convinced.

I checked my watch. "I should go."

"Yeah." Reaching over, Amy took my hand for a second and squeezed it, then let go. "I'll see you around, Elliott."

"See you around," I echoed.

And just like that, my first proper long-term relationship was over and I was a free man. Of sorts.

Megan was standing outside the closed Santa's grotto when I arrived, no longer dressed entirely in green felt and bells, although her blond hair was still tied back into two long plaits hanging either side of her face. Staring at her phone, flicking a finger across the screen with a frown every few moments, she didn't notice me until I was almost in front of her.

"No Becca?" I asked.

Megan looked up and smiled warmly. "She headed home with the shopping. *Somebody* stood her up, so she was in a foul mood anyway. Still want to grab some dinner?"

Bloody Sean. Could he not manage to not screw up, just for one day?

"Yeah, I guess."

Megan frowned. "What's up?"

"Nothing."

"Yeah, right. You look like you did the day Sean dropped your hamster and broke its back and it had to be put down. What happened?"

Megan could always read me too well. "Amy and I broke up."

"Oh. Sorry." Meg bit her lip. "Is that my fault? I mean, is it because of … this?"

"Partly." I gave a half shrug. "Partly not. But it's for the best, anyway."

"Sure?"

"Mostly."

"OK."

We stood in silence for a moment, looking out over the shoppers rushing around doing their Christmas shopping. I'd barely even thought about Christmas. All my focus was on January fifth and what happened after that.

"You know what I think?" Megan asked, then carried on without waiting for an answer. "I think Amy was part of your practice life. Like being a stupid elf is part of mine. We're both just getting ready for our real lives to start when we get to London."

"I just worry I'm wasting my time. That thinking about grand future plans is pointless. That what will actually happen is I'll get into loads of debt doing a useless degree and end up moving back home with my mum anyway."

"Well, we just won't let that happen." She sounded so sure, so convinced, I almost believed her. I suspected that Meg had never doubted that her dreams could come true.

I wished I had that kind of confidence.

Megan slipped a hand through my arm, perilously close to the ring in my pocket. "Come on. Let's go and get the bus home. We can pick up fish and chips from Sawyers. Just like we used to. Remember?"

"I remember." Back when Megan was just the girl next door, my dad still loved my mum and life was easy.

God, I missed those days.

BECCA
So, when you said you'd meet me this afternoon, that was what? A joke?

SEAN
Sorry. Got the chance to go out on the boats this afternoon.

BECCA
And you couldn't manage a text?

SEAN
No reception. Just got back ten minutes ago.

BECCA
Fine. Guess I know where I come in order of importance now. Beer, mates, sleep, boats and then somewhere way down at the bottom, Becca.

SEAN
Hey, come on. We agreed this was just a casual thing. I wasn't even supposed to be home this weekend. I only came to see you. That's got to count for something, right?

BECCA
Maybe. If you'd actually, I don't know, shown up to see me?

SEAN
Yeah. Right. Sorry again.

SEAN
Look, the truth is, I was trying to help Elliott out. He's doing his best and he'd already worked a shift this morning, but I know they're struggling at home without my pay cheque. So when I bumped into Jay this morning and he asked if I was free to help out... I figured the money was more important.

SEAN
Sorry.

BECCA
I suppose I get that.

SEAN
So I'm forgiven?

BECCA
Oh, I think you need to come up with a little more than that for forgiveness...

Megan

The plan was coming together. Becca's file of paperwork, plans and lists grew bigger every day. She'd hidden it under the paper bags on the counter shelf in Oracle, along with the copy of the relevant section of the will I'd managed to get Mum's solicitor to send me by pretending to be her secretary. Elliott had looked very relieved when we'd shown him the proof for our plan right there in black and white.

We'd managed to find a suitable dress reasonably quickly that Saturday. Possibly I was more easily persuaded because anything looked better on me than the stupid elf costume. But I was happy with it. A white knee-length dress, with a white and silver lace overlay. I guessed it was probably meant more for winter parties than weddings. But with my fluffy white cardigan and some silver heels, I figured it would do the job nicely. And, most importantly, it was cheap – fifty per cent off in the pre-Christmas sale. I didn't want to spend more of my elf money than necessary on non-essentials.

The next item on Becca's list was setting the scene with the parents. Mine were already questioning why I needed a part-time job when I should be using every second of my spare time to study for A levels. I'd managed to swing it by saying it was to help pay for Christmas presents. I just hoped they didn't get suspicious when they opened their usual cheapo presents from the Boots 3-for-2 offer.

But Christmas was the least of my worries. More importantly, I needed to sell my parents on being away for long enough to get to Gretna and back.

We'd figured we needed to be away two full days as a minimum. Taking Elliott's 'hiking in the Brecons' excuse, Becca had knocked up an official-looking letter on faked college headed paper, along with a permission slip at the bottom. Thank God the college had never really got to grips with the electronic update system, beyond basic information like school closures. I'd wanted to go for something more academic, like a history trip to London, but Elliott pointed out that would be the sort of overnight trip my parents might actually be interested in. Anything that would contribute towards my studies would lead to questions about itineraries and even – God forbid – volunteering to chaperone.

No. It needed to be the sort of thing that would make my parents' eyes glaze over but they'd let me go along because extra-curricular activities would look good on my UCAS application.

Now I just had to convince my parents that I was desperate to go out walking in the mountains in January. How hard could that be?

"Hiking?" Dad's brow wrinkled as he stared at the permission form. At least he didn't seem to be doubting the authenticity of the paperwork – just my willingness to participate. Even Lizzie, who'd taken part in basically every school activity going, had drawn the line at hiking. "You want to go on a hiking trip. Why?"

Fortunately, Elliott had given me a brilliant idea for this one when we'd picked up the forms. He'd predicted my parents' scepticism better than I had.

"It counts towards our grade for general studies somehow." Keep it vague. Dad had no idea how general studies worked, any more than anyone else did. "And, you know, that always looks good on university application forms."

That caught his attention, just as I'd known it would.

His focus shifted from the form to my face, searching, I assumed, for some evidence that I was really ready to live life the way they wanted me to.

I tried to look trustworthy and honest. Actually I tried to look like Lizzie.

"You've been thinking about where you want to apply, then?" Dad asked, not even trying to hide the eagerness in his voice. "And are you thinking for this year or next? Because if you're going to switch over to Woolten Academy and repeat the year, you've got a bit more time to build up your evidence base for your application. I imagine they might have some better opportunities than hiking in the Brecons in winter."

"I figure it's a good idea to keep my options open," I said lightly. "And this way I'm maximizing my potential for getting a place where I want, regardless of what I decide to do about resitting the year." All true, really. I was making sure I got to London in September, or sooner, because there wasn't a chance in hell of me resitting my A level year.

"That's a sensible way of looking at it." Dad nodded sagely as he spoke. "And while you're thinking about your options, perhaps it would be helpful for us to sit down and talk them through? Help you see the advantages of Woolten, for a start?"

"Sorry, I can't. I'm meeting Becca." I flashed him a smile and made a grab for my coat, hoping Dad wouldn't ask why I was heading out so early – it was barely five thirty. I was glad I'd caught him in the hallway, as close as possible to several escape routes. "You'll sign the form, yeah?"

"If that's what you want," Dad said, still holding the slightly crumpled piece of paper in his hands. "What time will you be home?"

"The usual," I sang out, already halfway out of the door. "See ya."

The front door slammed behind me and I was free.

The only problem was, I'd been lying about seeing Becca – after a day of ignoring my texts, she'd finally replied to say that she had other plans. Which I assumed meant that Sean was down. Again.

At some point she was going to have to stop distracting me with wedding plans every time I asked her what was going on there. But for now, it just meant I had nowhere to go. And the December air was pretty damn chilly. I paused as I reached the main street, looking out over the freezing waves, and weighed up my options. I could see if anyone I knew was out in the pubs but it was too early and, besides, Wednesday evening wasn't usually the most fun of nights out. I could go and gatecrash Becca and Sean's date.

Or I could go and spend some time with my husband-to-be.

Decision made, I shoved my hands in my coat pockets for warmth and headed towards the dodgier side of town.

Elliott

My UCAS application was complete.

I leaned back in my chair and considered the form as a whole, spread out across my desk in its final, printed-out-for-reading-through version. I'd give it one last double-check for spelling but otherwise … it was done.

That document symbolized my one shot at getting the future I'd dreamed of as a kid, and the more time I spent with Megan the more real the dream was becoming. In fact, it wasn't even symbolic. It *was* my chance. Whoever read that application, I just had to hope and pray they liked it enough to offer me a place on the course I wanted. Otherwise, this whole wedding thing was for nothing. My grades were good enough and I'd worked hard on the form. The rest … that was probably down to luck.

The form and the ring sitting in its paper bag on my shelf were my dreams made solid. I'd made my choices, burned my bridges and set my plans.

But I was still too scared to press 'Apply'.

I couldn't shake the feeling that there were too many things that could go wrong. Megan was going all out for this wedding and I believed she really wanted it. But everything had changed so fast to get us here, I couldn't quite move past the possibility of it changing back.

No. I'd have to wait until that ring was firmly on her finger before I sent in the form. It was the only way I could be sure.

There was a knock and before I could call out for Mum to come in, my bedroom door opened and Megan's blond curls appeared around it, followed by the rest of her.

"Hey, future husband," she said, too loudly to be considered even vaguely stealthy.

"Oh, for God's sake!" I jumped up and shut the door, just in case my mum was loitering outside. The last thing I needed was her getting suspicious at this late stage. "Can you just ... not?"

Megan sat on my bed. "What? Ashamed of me?"

I rolled my eyes. "Do you really want my mum asking questions about our plans for the future?"

"No," Megan admitted. "Especially since I've just been discussing the very same with my dad. He's going to sign the permission slip. Though it's not like anyone's going to be checking."

I sat back down at my desk. "Do you ever get a bit confused as to what's real and what isn't in this plan?"

Megan shook her head, hair swishing around her face. "I just focus on the end result and figure the rest will all fall into place."

Maybe that was how she managed to be so relaxed, when I was freaking out every minute of the day.

Getting to her feet, Megan crossed my room to stand beside me, flicking idly through a few of my university prospectuses as if they were magazines.

"Huh." She paused in her flicking, staring at the open page. "A BA in photography. Who knew that was even a thing?"

"You can study pretty much anything, if you're willing to pay the fees." I wanted to close the prospectus, to snatch them all away from her and hide them. It was weird enough having Megan in my room again after so many years. And these days... Well, we weren't ten any more.

"So, what made you want to be a photographer in the first place?" I asked, searching for a way to make this feel more normal. Had she even said why she'd come over in the first place? What did she want?

Meg shrugged. "I'm good at it – that was the starting point, I guess. I mean, when I began taking photos it was a distraction, something to think about that wasn't Lizzie. But it grew into so much more than that... I love it. I like capturing a moment in time, so people can hold on to it forever. I like catching that split second that no one else even notices – that glance, that smile, that crest of a wave ... everything." She bit her lip and I knew she was weighing up whether to say something more, so I waited. "It's like ... memories matter, you know? The photos people took of Lizzie ... they're all we have left now, really."

She looked away, fiddling with the model boat she'd found on my desk – one that Sean had offloaded into my room but wouldn't let me get rid of. An awkward silence stretched between us and I wondered if she was regretting saying what she had about Lizzie. I changed the subject, hoping it would shift the frown from Megan's face.

"You've been doing it a while, then?" When she first mentioned it, I'd just assumed this was another of Megan's whims. But having watched her over the last month and seen the lengths she was willing to go to, I knew it was something more. Maybe Meg had found her passion at last.

"Over a year," she said. "Since Lizzie died. I mostly do seascapes and still lifes – the sort of thing you see in travel magazines and glossy books. I've been talking with Elodie at the Seashell Gallery about selling some of my prints. But I think she wants more people shots, instead." She turned to me, the boat still in her hand. "I'm good, Elliott. And this isn't something I'm just going to give up on if it gets hard."

"I didn't say—"

"But you were thinking it." She sighed. "I don't just jump from one thing to the next any more."

"I know that. You wouldn't be marrying me if you weren't serious. Would you?" I asked, eyebrows raised. She pulled a face.

"No. So … good. Because I'm as serious about this as you are about archaeology. Speaking of which…" She pulled a loose piece of paper from the UCL prospectus. "Why are you here?"

I blinked. "I'm pretty sure that's the question I should have asked you the minute you appeared."

"*I'm* here because Becca is probably off somewhere with your brother and I'm avoiding my parents," she explained. "But *you* should be on your way to Swansea right now."

She held up the piece of paper and my eyes scanned

over the text. Dr Robert Forrest from UCL was giving a series of lectures across the UK, talking about some of the latest digs and research going on at the university.

I took it from her.

"He's talking in Swansea? Tonight?"

"Starts in an hour and a half." She looked at me, studying my face. "Did Sean leave his car here?"

"I think so. Why?"

"Because we could still make it if we leave now."

Just jump in the car and drive to Swansea. No plans, no googling directions or finding out if there were any tickets left. That wasn't the way Megan did things. She didn't worry about consequences, or what people might say, or what could go wrong.

No wonder Becca was planning our elopement for us.

"We?" I asked.

Meg shrugged. "It's not like I have anything better to do tonight. So, come on. Are we going?"

I thought about it, trying to be quick enough that Meg wouldn't get bored of the idea and wander off. After all, this wasn't her passion, it was mine. And I'd buried it so deep, I'd almost forgotten about it until she reminded me.

I didn't want to let it go again.

So, I could go and see Dr Robert Forrest talking,

155

in person. I could be spontaneous. I could spend the evening with Megan.

"OK then," I said, grabbing my wallet from the desk. "Let's go."

Megan clapped her hands and beamed. "Road trip!"

Megan

We were cutting it fine, even with Elliott driving, and we were very nearly late for the lecture. But fortunately the lecture theatre wasn't too far from the car park so we were able to slip in the back and find seats just as the lights were dimming.

Dr Robert Forrest, it turned out, was younger than I'd expected – like, forties instead of seventies – and kind of hot in an older film star way. But more than that, he was *engaging*. He made archaeology into stories, telling one anecdote that flowed into another, punctuated by jokes and asides that kept the audience listening. Even me, with my total lack of interest in the subject.

What was even more interesting, though, was watching Elliott listen to the lecture.

I knew that this was kind of a big deal to him. But I hadn't realized how obsessed he still was with the subject. He was like me about photography, I'd just never seen it before.

His gaze never moved from Dr Forrest pacing around the stage but somehow he managed to keep scribbling notes and questions in the small black notebook he'd pulled from his pocket when we arrived, turning the page whenever he reached the end without even looking. Half the questions didn't even make sense to me but I could tell the ones that mattered most to Elliott. They were the ones that had been underlined three times or had a star marked next to them. For someone who claimed to have given up on his dream, he'd jumped back in as soon as he'd been given the opportunity.

Maybe Elliott hadn't changed quite as much as I'd thought. Then I glanced over at him again and knew that wasn't true. The fluttery feeling I got inside if I looked at him for too long told me that much, even if I was trying to ignore it.

"And that, guys, is why I became an archaeologist." Dr Forrest finished his lecture with a flourish, to enthusiastic applause. Elliott clapped louder than anybody and I belatedly joined in. "So, any questions?"

There were lots. Some were about career planning, some about degree courses, some about digs and research he'd undertaken.

But nobody had asked the question that had the most underlines and stars in Elliott's notebook. He tapped his pen against it as Dr Forrest talked but showed no sign of putting his hand up.

It dawned on me that he never did. Not in history class, even when I knew he knew the answers. Never in any college assemblies or meetings, or even in smaller seminar groups. Elliott didn't volunteer anything. Didn't offer any answers or opinions, ever.

Why was that? Was it that he didn't think anyone would listen? Because that was awful.

I nudged him in the ribs and, when he still didn't do anything, lifted his hand up into the air for him.

Elliott stared at me with wide eyes, for so long that he almost missed Dr Forrest saying, "Yes? At the back?"

I elbowed Elliott again and he swallowed before stuttering out the first words of his question.

"Right. Well, I was wondering…" He paused, took a breath and started again. "You talked a lot about your personal reasons for following a career in archaeology but I was wondering… What role do you see for archaeologists in the world today, especially with the ongoing destruction of some of the world's oldest and most valuable sites in the Middle East?"

Dr Forrest smiled broadly. "*That* is an excellent

question. And one I'd actually like to put to you. You're hoping to have a career as an archaeologist, right? What role do you see for yourself in that world?"

The whole audience had turned round now to stare at Elliott. I bit my lip as I waited to hear his answer. Did he even have one? Until last month he'd given up on ever studying archaeology at all. And now he had to define his career path? That was a big ask.

But this was also his chance. Dr Forrest was based at UCL according to his bio – that was Elliott's top choice university. If he gave the right answer now, he could sail into a great offer as soon as his UCAS form was submitted. Well, he could once I'd dragged him down to the front to introduce himself to Dr Forrest.

Elliott had gone along with my crazy plan, every step of the way, with hardly any wobbles. The least I could do was give him a push towards his dream career.

"I think there's a lot of work to be done, recovering what is lost and protecting what we still have – as well as making new discoveries," Elliott said finally. "And I want to be a part of that. I want future generations to be able to study sites and artefacts through the new technologies that are being developed. I think archaeology needs to be looking backwards *and* forwards."

Dr Forrest nodded enthusiastically. "I agree. I think that's exactly the way the next generation of archaeologists – that's you guys – needs to be thinking. And that's a great note to end the night on. Thanks, everyone!"

The lecture theatre filled with rustles and chatter as people got to their feet and gathered their stuff. Elliott started to stand but I tugged on his arm to pull him back down.

"We're not going?" he asked, confused.

"Not yet," I said. "First you need to go and introduce yourself to Dr Forrest."

"What? Why?" Down at the front of the hall, Dr Forrest had already been swamped by enthusiastic audience members. We didn't want to be one of those; we could wait our turn. But Elliott was definitely talking to the man.

"Because he basically said that you're exactly what the field of archaeology needs. So you need to go and tell him your name, so that when your UCAS form comes across his desk he recognizes it and offers you a place at UCL."

Elliott blinked. "You think?"

"I know." Dr Forrest had started making his way out of the gaggle of fans. Time to go. "Come on."

We caught up with him by the doors.

"Dr Forrest?" Elliott said, at my prompting. Dr Forrest turned and smiled at us. "Um, I just wanted to say thanks for a great talk."

"And thank you for a great question." He eyed Elliott speculatively. "Are you already studying for an archaeology degree?"

Elliott shook his head. "Just applying this year. UCL is top of my list."

"Glad to hear it. What's your name?"

"Elliott Redwood."

Dr Forrest pulled an identical notebook to Elliott's from his pocket and scribbled it down. I rolled my eyes. Apparently even Elliott's choice in stationery made him destined to become an archaeologist. "Mention this lecture on your form. I don't want to miss the opportunity to have you studying with us next year." He held out a hand to Elliott.

"I will." Elliott shook his hand enthusiastically. "Thank you."

"See you in October, Elliott Redwood." And with that, Dr Forrest disappeared through the doors, leaving Elliott and me alone in the empty lecture theatre.

"That was ... awesome." Elliott turned and beamed at me. "Thanks."

I shrugged. "All you needed was a little prodding. Or nagging."

Elliott laughed. "Imagine what you'll be able to talk me into when we're married, then."

"I'm already making a list," I joked. "Starting with – get up behind that lectern."

"What?" Elliott blinked at me, so I gave him a little shove towards the stage. He staggered forwards obediently and stood in the same spot Dr Forrest had to begin his talk. I pulled out my phone and snapped a few shots of him standing there.

"Pretend like you're giving a lecture."

Elliott rolled his eyes but turned and pointed to the screen anyway. Laughing, I took some more photos, before dropping my phone back into my pocket.

"Perfect," I said. "I'll save those for when you become a proper professor or whatever. I can tell people I always knew you'd do it."

Elliott laughed. "Come on. We'd better get home before Sean notices we nicked his car for the night." Jumping down from the stage, he grabbed his bag and jacket from where he'd placed them on the floor. "But seriously, Meg?" I turned to find him watching me. "Thank you. I'd given up, you know? And without you … I'd have no chance at this at all."

I glanced away, suddenly awkward.

"You're welcome," I said. "No reason we can't live our dreams together, right?"

"As long as we can make it to Gretna and back without anyone noticing."

"Piece of cake," I told him. Even though, inside, the days between now and January fifth seemed to loom long and full of potential dangers.

Just twenty-one days to go.

The countdown was on.

SEAN
Does this mean I've made it up to you for the other week?

BECCA
I think you might just have done, actually.

SEAN
But you're not completely sure? Because if you're not sure, I'll just have to do it again. Soon.

BECCA
In that case, I'm not at all sure... How long are you home for?

SEAN
Already broken up for Christmas. I'm here all the way through to mid-January.

BECCA
That's a lot of time for making up. I mean, if you want to.

SEAN
Well, I'd hate to still owe you or anything...

BECCA
Then maybe we can make up again. Soon.

SEAN
Definitely soon.

Elliott

Christmas used to be kind of a big deal at our house. Before everything happened with Dad, I mean. These days, Mum was usually working late in The Anchor on Christmas Eve, often after working all day at the supermarket. I figured Sean and I would assemble some sort of Christmas dinner from ready meals the next day to give her a break.

Sean had been home from university for a couple of weeks and, by the time we got to Christmas Eve, the house was already feeling too small. Mum had spent the week since school broke up pestering me about university. "Now's the perfect time to get your applications sorted, Elliott, while you're not busy with college and there's not much work. You haven't got long until they're due in, remember. And I know you say you're not going to go but really, love, what's the harm in keeping your options open? Just apply. For me."

I just nodded non-committally. Part of me wanted to tell her that I already had my application ready to go, just to get her off my back. But another part – the part that wouldn't let me press send until January sixth – didn't want to get her hopes up. Just in case.

Because in Mum's mind, all I had to do was send in a form and my future was secure. She didn't think about things like fees and loans and rent and debt that never got paid off. In her mind, she worked hard enough for everything else to be easy and university was the opportunity that meant I wouldn't have to work like her. I hoped she was right ... but I still knew it was a risk. University didn't mean a guaranteed job any more – just guaranteed debt.

Mum let the door slam in the wind as she headed out to her shift in the pub, one last reminder about how I *could* spend my evening ringing in my ears. Sean, fresh from the shower and with his hair dripping, leaned over and clapped a hand on my shoulder, sending droplets of water down my collar.

"Oh, cheers." I pulled away.

"Just forget about it tonight," Sean suggested. "All of it. Let's go down the cove."

The cove on Christmas Eve was *our* tradition. We'd been going there since long before we were old enough to go out on Christmas Eve. When we were little kids, we'd take a walk on the beach with Mum and Dad every Christmas Eve morning before we headed off to spend Christmas with Dad's family in Birmingham. Then, when we were a bit older, Sean and I would meet up with Lizzie and Megan at the cove on Christmas Eve afternoon, when our parents were busy getting everything ready for the next day, and have our own celebration. Lizzie would save the chocolates from her advent calendar all month then share them out between us, Sean would nick all the chocolates off the Christmas tree to add in and we'd gorge ourselves until we got too cold and had to head home.

Nowadays it was more likely to be half a bottle of vodka to ward off the chill.

"The cove? Let me guess – Becca's going to be there." Sean was still being cagey about exactly what was going on with him and Becca. But I'd caught them on the sofa at our house the other day, so I had an unfortunate mental image of what they were spending their time doing.

"And Megan." Sean waggled his eyebrows at me. "Anything you want to confess to there?"

"Nothing at all," I said, and went to grab my coat.

"You know," Sean said as we headed down the street to the beach. "The university thing—"

I groaned. "I thought we were forgetting about it for tonight?"

"Yeah, but after this, right? I was just thinking … you could ask Dad. For the money, I mean. Last time I was there—"

"You visited him again?" I stopped walking and stared at him.

"Said I was going to, didn't I?"

"No."

Sean sighed. "Look, he's still Dad, OK. And yeah. I'm still mad at him, too. But he's sorry. And he's the only dad we've got."

"I'd rather go without, thanks." I turned away and headed for the beach.

"Yeah, well, that's stupid," Sean said, catching me up. "He's still got some money put by, you see."

"Other people's money."

Sean hesitated at that. "Yeah, probably, to be honest. But he has it. And given what he put us through… Don't you think you deserve some of it? To get out there and find a life away from this godforsaken place."

"I don't need his help. I'll find my own way."

"What? Working the boats for the rest of your life?" Sean scoffed.

It was on the tip of my tongue to tell him everything.

To tell him that I'd found a way out that didn't involve selling my soul to the Navy or to Dad.

But I didn't. We were nearly there. The last thing we needed now was Sean's big gob ruining everything.

"Just leave it, yeah?" I said, rubbing a hand over my eyes. "It's Christmas. So just … leave it."

Sean slung an arm round my shoulder. "Yeah, all right. Let's just go and get plastered."

Finally a plan I could get behind.

Megan

For the first time ever, the Christmas holidays dragged. I couldn't think about presents or focus on decorating the tree or smiling nicely at Mum and Dad's acquaintances during their annual festive drinks party. All I could think about was January fifth. My wedding day. My day of freedom.

And it was still ages away.

Christmas Eve meant a party at the cove, as usual. Mostly I was just glad to be escaping my parents, whose questions about university applications and Woolten Academy were growing more pointed.

"So, is Sean coming tonight?" I asked Becca as we walked down the beach towards the cove, coats wrapped tight around us.

She shrugged. "Probably. He didn't say for definite." I had to lean in to hear her over the crashing waves.

"Really? Then what were you guys texting about

earlier?" Becca had come round to get ready at mine and had barely looked up from her phone the whole time, even when I was taking her photo for the end-of-year collage I had planned.

She blushed. "I might have been texting someone else."

"No, you weren't."

"No, I wasn't," she agreed.

"So, what were you talking about?"

Becca shrugged and shoved her hands in the pockets of her coat. "Just stuff. He's worried about Elliott. About him not applying to university. I told him not to worry—"

"Becca, you can't tell him," I cut in, a chill going through me that had nothing to do with the December cold.

"I'm not going to, idiot." She bumped her elbow against my side. "As I was about to say – but obviously I couldn't explain to him how I knew Elliott would be OK. I haven't come this far to spill all your secrets now."

"Right. Sorry." Relief flowed through me just as the campfires came into sight and the sound of partying drowned out the waves.

"What are those idiots doing?" Becca stopped walking, staring up at the rocks at the far end of the cove. I followed her gaze and saw the figures of five boys climbing up them, dark shadows against the rock. "Is that Dylan?"

"And Evan." I could barely get the words out. Because I could already guess what they were doing. What we all used to do in the summer – climb up high enough when the tide was in and jump into the waves. It was stupid and dangerous in the daylight and in the warmth of summer. In the dark, in winter, it was positively lethal.

I might not have much time for Dylan or his brother and his friends any more but I was damned if I'd let anyone else die off this cove because Evan Roberts got drunk and stupid.

They were laughing, nearly at the top of the rocks now – an almost completely sheer cliff face above the water. Panic surged through me, throbbing in my veins. I had to stop them. Dashing forwards, I shouted up at them but my words were whipped away by the wind, leaving me screaming at nothing.

"You idiots!" I shrieked, but the boys didn't turn, didn't react. Didn't hear.

"What's going on?" Elliott's cool, even voice did nothing to calm me down. I spun towards him, shaking, and he grabbed my arms to hold me still.

"What's the matter?"

I yanked my arm free to point up at the rocks behind me. But before I could find the words to explain, Elliott had already figured it out.

"OK. Stay here." He let go of my other arm and moved past me, striding purposefully towards the cliffs.

"What are you going to do?" I called. But he was already gone. Moments later he was scrambling up the rocks towards Dylan and his mates and I lurched forwards again to stop him. The last thing tonight needed was Elliott getting into a fight with Evan – especially up on the cliffs. It was too easy for someone to fall.

But I should have known Elliott better than that. As I stood at the bottom of the rocks, the wind dropped for a moment. Elliott, halfway up, pulled a phone from his pocket.

"Oi!" he yelled. "Idiots!"

Holding out the phone to show them, he shouted up to a jeering Dylan just as the wind rose again. I only caught half his words after that but it was enough.

Elliott was threatening to call the police. Just like he'd done the night Evan stole the boat and took Lizzie out on the water.

"Get down ... call ... police. You ... do it, too."

Elliott's words were whipped away on the wind but from their response, it seemed like Dylan and the others heard enough.

The heckling only grew louder but I could see Freddie shaking his head in the moonlight. "Not worth it," he yelled, taking the first steps back down.

My heart started to beat again as, one by one, the boys descended the rocks. Elliott jumped down ahead of them, stalking away – past me, past where Becca stood with Sean. I guessed he didn't want to be in the line of fire when Dylan and Evan made it down.

I didn't blame him. Sober, they were idiots. Drunk, they were dangerous.

Once I was sure everyone was safely down, I turned and followed Elliott.

I found him standing on the edge of the furthest of the three campfires, watching Amy and his friends singing along to the guitars. Biting my lip, I stepped up beside him.

"Thanks."

He shook his head. "You're not the one who should be thanking me. They could have broken their stupid necks."

"Yeah, but they're not going to thank you. So I will. I should have thought of calling the police." If anyone had called, that would have been the end of the cove as a place to meet, for a while at least.

"It's basically become my trademark move," Elliott joked, but he didn't sound very amused by it.

"Do you wish you were over there tonight?" I asked, nodding at Amy.

He took a moment then shook his head, turning to smile at me instead. "No. In fact, I don't really want to be here at all."

"Want to take a walk?" I suggested.

"Yeah," Elliott said, with one last look back at the rocks. "Let's get out of here."

Elliott

"I can't believe you ever went out with him," I said as we followed the bend around the cliffs and the noise of the cove faded away behind us.

"Dylan?" Megan's nose wrinkled up as she pulled a face. She looked pale beside me in the mix of moonlight and the yellow cast of the street lamps from the road above. "Me, neither."

"Why did you?"

She shrugged. "Honestly? I'm not sure. I mean, he was fairly obvious about liking me and we had a laugh together. We were all hanging out most of the time anyway. It just sort of … happened. But I can't tell you why. It's like I was a different person then."

"Before Lizzie."

"Yeah." Megan's steps slowed a little. "I was with him, you know. The night she died. And afterwards … I couldn't even look at him."

I didn't reply to that. What could I say? That I knew where she'd been that night because Lizzie had told me? How would that help now?

"Come on," I said. "I know where we should go."

I led her further down the beach, all the way past the harbour to where the brightly coloured tourist cottages clustered around the beach. They were mostly dark, now, although one or two of them had lights on – families spending Christmas away from home, I supposed.

At the far edge, a path led up to the old viewing platform, a leftover from when St Evaline was a seaside town favoured by the Edwardians. These days, all that was left was a bench with a brass plaque and a telescope that took 20p pieces.

We sat on the bench, close enough to share warmth, and looked out over the waves in silence. After a long moment, Megan tipped her head to rest it against my shoulder and, automatically, I stretched out an arm round her.

It felt like she was exactly where she should be.

At least until she said, "Will you tell me about Lizzie?"

My shoulders stiffened. "You knew her better than I did."

"I don't mean her, generally. I meant…"

"Her last night." Because hadn't I known she'd ask eventually?

"Yeah."

I sighed and shifted, taking my arm back, and Megan sat up again, staring at me and waiting for my answer.

"You've already heard it all. In my testimony."

"That was just the facts," Megan pointed out. "I want to know … how she looked. How she felt. What she was thinking."

"I don't think she was, much," I admitted. "She was drunk before I even got to the cove that night."

"That's the part I don't understand. Lizzie hardly ever drank – and when she did, she didn't get drunk. I don't get why she would – or why she was with Evan Roberts."

"Maybe she just wanted to party after her exams," I suggested, knowing it wasn't the truth. "She'd just finished her AS levels, right?"

"And aced them." Megan smiled. "Just like we knew she would. The school sent the results on to us, after. She wanted to apply to Oxbridge, you know. She'd have got in, too, if she'd…"

The word Megan couldn't say hung in the icy air between us.

"So, she was celebrating?" Megan said, after a pause. "I guess that's something. She was happy. She died happy."

She looked up at me, waiting for confirmation, and I knew I couldn't tell her the truth. Not yet. It would break her heart to know what Lizzie had really been thinking that night. And I couldn't do that to her – not when it wouldn't change anything anyway. Lizzie would still be dead.

I didn't want Megan to blame herself, the way I did.

"I'm sorry I couldn't stop her getting on that boat," I said softly, and Megan shook her head.

"It wasn't your fault. I shouldn't have blamed you."

How could you? How could you let her go like that? I trusted you, Elliott! I trusted you to look after her. Megan's words from that awful morning after echoed through my brain.

"You were right. You trusted me to look after her." Not that she'd asked or anything. But it was implicit. Lizzie was always the good one, the naïve one, the one who needed protecting from people who might lead her astray, for all that she was older than us. Me and Megan might not have been as close as we were as kids by then but that basic truth still stood. We all looked after Lizzie. "If Sean had been there…"

"But he wasn't," Megan said. "And even if he had been, it might not have made a difference. Lizzie could be stubborn when she'd made her mind up about something."

You can't stop me, Elliott. This is my *choice. One I'm making for myself, for once. Like Megan would.*

I shook Lizzie's words away. There was no use remembering them now.

Overhead the stars twinkled in the clear black sky, reflected in the rolling waters below.

"Is that ... is that why you agreed to do all this?" Megan asked, her voice hesitant. "Because of Lizzie?"

"No." She stared at me until I had to look away. "Maybe to start with. But now..." I caught her gaze again and held it, so she'd know I was telling the truth. "Now I want this for myself. You reminded me of all the things I wanted once. And you gave me a way to get them."

"You will get them," Megan promised, grabbing my hands tight. "We both will."

Behind us, the church clock chimed twelve, the bells ringing out in the night. It was Christmas morning.

I smiled. "Merry Christmas, Megan."

Megan

Christmas was the usual mess of overcooked sprouts and bad movies. It was our second Christmas without Lizzie but we still hadn't figured out how to deal with the hole at the heart of our celebrations. So instead we just pretended it was an ordinary day, only with presents and turkey, and me snapping photos of us opening gifts and pulling crackers.

But nothing felt ordinary, this year.

The days dragged on between Christmas and New Year and I willed them to pass faster, knowing each hour brought me closer to my wedding day.

By New Year's Eve I was going stir-crazy. Becca had said to meet her at some pub we never went to – I suspected because it was a favourite of Sean's. It was as good a way to kill time as any, so I pulled on an appropriately sparkly dress, did something with my hair and applied slightly more make-up than normal.

I passed through the kitchen, grabbing a glass of water to hydrate before the alcohol, and glanced in passing at the stack of papers on the end of the counter.

Then I looked again, pulling out the one with mine and Lizzie's names on it that was peeking out halfway down.

There was a covering letter from the solicitor – the same headed paper I recognized from my request for a copy of Grandma Alice's will – apologizing for the inclusion of Lizzie's name and mentioning that apparently the developer had been working from older documents.

Wait. Developer?

Quickly, I read the enclosed letter, heat and fury rising within me with every word.

"Megan, do you need a lift into town?" Dad asked. I looked up at him, eyes blazing.

"Were you even going to tell me about this?" I waved the letter at him, already knowing the answer. The letter was dated three weeks ago. If they were going to tell me, they would have already done it.

Dad sighed. "Meg, it's boring solicitor business. I didn't honestly think you'd be interested."

"Not interested in someone wanting to buy *my* flat?"

As if. Even if I hadn't had big plans for it, it was still my business.

"It's not yours until you turn twenty-one." My mother appeared in the kitchen doorway behind Dad and looked me up and down. "Where are you going dressed like that?"

"It's mine. You're only supposed to be holding it in trust for me. Not selling it to the highest bidder without consulting me!"

"That's not—" Dad started, but Mum spoke over him, pushing past to stand in front of him.

"That's exactly what we're supposed to do – if it's in your best interests. That's the whole point of the trust! We look after it until you are deemed adult enough to take care of it yourself – which at the rate you're going, will be never." Mum folded her arms and looked ready to continue, until Dad put a hand on her shoulder and caught her eye as she looked up.

"Look, let's sit down and talk about this sensibly," he said.

"Why?" I asked. "You've obviously already decided I can't be trusted to have any input at all into my own future." This, right here, was *exactly* why I needed to marry Elliott and get the hell out of St Evaline.

"Please, Megan." Dad used his best 'patient dad'

expression and I gave in. After all, I needed to get more information on exactly what the deal was here before I could find a way to stop it.

We all moved through to the lounge, where I took up defensive positioning in the armchair closest to the door and waited for them to explain.

"OK, so, as you saw, a developer has been in touch with the solicitor about buying Grandma Alice's flat," Dad started.

"Why?" I asked. I mean, I knew why *I* wanted the flat but, as I remembered it, it wasn't anything special. Not to anyone who hadn't known and loved Grandma Alice. Why would a developer be interested?

"The area is undergoing a bit of a renaissance," Dad said. "New shops are opening all the time and property prices are rocketing."

I didn't care about new shops. I cared about losing my escape route.

"We received this offer a few weeks ago and we've been discussing it since."

"Without me."

Mum ignored my interruption. "I don't know if you remember, but Grandma Alice's flat is the ground floor of an old Victorian terrace that's been split in two."

"I remember," I said shortly. I remembered every single thing about that flat, from the sunny yellow kitchen to the exposed wooden floorboards, the dreamcatchers hanging in the bedroom windows to the way the back door stuck whenever you went out into the tiny back garden.

"Anyway, it's not in great shape. Our management company has already told us the flat is going to need some significant work if we want to be able to rent it out to young professionals rather than students. But the developer is willing to buy it as is. He's looking to acquire both the flats in the house and return it to a family home again, since that's what the area is crying out for," Dad explained. "He's willing to put up some serious money."

"But it's not Grandma Alice's flat any more," I pointed out. "She left it to me and Lizzie, and now it's just mine. And I don't want to sell it." If they'd actually *talked* to me about my future instead of making decisions for me, they'd have known that.

Mum and Dad exchanged one of *those* looks. The ones that told me they were wondering how they managed to have a child as stupid as me.

"I'm not sure you fully understand the opportunity here," Mum said with exaggerated patience. "We can afford to pay for you to resit your A level year at Woolten Academy but that money will have to come from your college fund. The money the developer is offering would mean you wouldn't have to take out a student loan to pay for your studies at Oxford or Cambridge and you'd even have enough left for a deposit on a house somewhere more practical." She pushed a piece of paper with a frankly unbelievable figure on it towards me. I ignored it. The money mattered less than the principle. Once the flat was mine, I could choose to sell if I wanted. I knew London prices were ridiculous but that flat was worth more to me as a place to live when I moved to London with Elliott.

"And if I wanted either of those things, maybe I'd consider it." Why couldn't they hear me? Was I speaking a foreign language? Had evolution made it impossible for teenagers and parents to communicate effectively?

"Besides, the decision isn't up to you," Mum went on. "Until you formally inherit the flat at twenty-one, your father and I are the final decision-makers. And the terms of the trust are very clear – if an offer is made over market value and if it's in your best interest to sell, we can do that."

"But it's not in my best interest! I don't want to sell!"

My calm, rational exterior was crumbling.

Dad sighed. "We're not going to steamroller you into this, Meg."

"Funny, that sounds exactly like what you're doing."

"We just want you to think about it," Mum added. "Think about the possibilities that kind of money would offer you."

"We've already set you up with an interview at Woolten Academy in the new year," Dad said. "The developer doesn't need a final answer for two more weeks. Why don't you think about it and see how you feel after you visit Woolten?"

"Two weeks?" In two weeks I'd be married and the flat would be mine. In two weeks they would have no power to make my decisions for me. In two weeks, none of this would matter at all.

"Yes," Dad said. "So you'll think about it?"

"I'll think about it," I promised. It wasn't a lie. I'd be thinking exactly how well I'd dodged this bullet when I said 'I do' in five days' time. "Is there anything else about my life you've been keeping from me? Only I told Becca I'd be there by now."

"That's all," Dad said. "Have fun. And don't be too late home, OK?"

"I won't. See you." I dashed out of the door before

Mum realized I'd never answered her question about where I was going.

Checking my watch I considered my options. I was already late to meet Becca. But given this latest development, I had one more stop I wanted to make on my way to the party.

Elliott

New Year had never been a really big thing for me, mostly because it was also the day my dad left. Mum turned down shifts at The Anchor, every year. She said she didn't want to go out and deal with people and I always felt too bad to leave her home alone. So when Sean mentioned a party at some pub, I shook my head and said I had better things to do than watch him and Becca pretending they weren't a couple all night.

"We're not!" he protested. "We're just … having fun."

"And that's why you've been home more this half term than all of last year?" I asked.

Sean winked. "Don't knock a bit of fun, just because you don't know how to have any!"

Then he was gone, off to get drunk and flirt and do all the things I wanted to be doing. Instead I was stuck at home worrying about the future – specifically, about what would happen in five days' time. I'd been putting off worrying about what would happen after the wedding – what my mum would say, or Sean – so I could focus on making our Gretna trip happen. If I thought too much about Mum's reaction or her listening to the town whispering about what that good-for-nothing son of hers had done now, I felt like I was drowning in reasons not to do it.

So I just didn't think about it. Making the marriage happen at all was enough worry for me.

And as it happened, I was worrying alone.

"I'm off out, El!" Mum called as I was halfway up the stairs. I stopped, turned and stared.

Mum, who mostly lived in jeans and cardigans, was wearing a dress. A black and red, close-fitting, low-cut dress. *And* she'd brushed her hair and put on make-up.

"You're going out?" I asked, even though I could see what the answer would be. *Of course* she was going out. Why else would she be all dressed up and telling me she was off?

"Yeah." Mum smiled down at her high-heeled shoes, a faint blush on her cheeks. "There's this guy I met when I was working down at The Anchor, he asked me out tonight."

"Well that's … great." I tried to sound more enthusiastic than surprised.

"You don't mind?" she asked. "I know we normally

spend tonight together but I thought you might be out with your brother this year... If you want me to stay, I can call and cancel."

"No! Definitely not." I smiled at her. "You should absolutely go out and have a brilliant night. I might go and catch up with Sean later anyway. Don't worry about me." Normally I'd have been with Amy and the others. But since the break-up, hanging out with them was a whole new level of awkward.

"If you're sure..." She was already halfway out of the door.

"I am," I assured her. "See you later."

The door shut behind her and I stood there, in the middle of the stairs, trying to figure out what to do next.

I could go out, I supposed. Some beers and a laugh with Sean could go a long way to distracting me from all the stuff spinning round my head. But a strange, sensible part of me remembered that big nights out in town usually involved someone getting too drunk to keep their voice down when talking about me and my family, or someone knocking into me and making a comment about my dad, or maybe some guy just looking for a fight. Normally I tried not to care that much. But with only five days to go ... I didn't want anything to jeopardize the plan. Before I could decide, someone knocked on the front door.

"Meg?" She was dressed in a short sparkly dress, showing far more of her legs than I was used to. Her hair was styled in perfect waves and her lips were a deep plummy colour. If it hadn't been for the scowl on her face, she'd have looked gorgeous.

Who am I kidding? She was gorgeous anyway. Gorgeous and seriously annoyed about something.

"Have you asked Sean about borrowing the car yet?"

Ah. The car. I'd been meaning to, but I wasn't quite sure how I was going to explain needing his car for two or three days. Especially since, as far as he and Mum knew, I'd be hiking in the Brecons at that exact same time. I never had been very good at lying – to anyone, really. But especially not to my big brother. Sean always saw through it.

Apparently my expression gave away the answer, as Meg pulled a face and made a frustrated noise. "You haven't. Great. Do you know how much train tickets will cost now we've left it this late? Not to mention it'll take us twice as long to get there. If we miss our slot…"

"I'll ask him, OK?" My irritation bled into my voice. I'd gone along with every bit of her plan so far. She didn't need to nag me.

"When?" Meg pressed. "We're leaving in four days, Elliott. You're running out of time."

"When I find the right moment," I snapped, but Megan shook her head.

"No. No excuses. We're going to go and ask him together. Right now." She grabbed my arm and yanked me out of the front door.

"Hang on!" I grabbed my keys and a coat from the rack just in time to be hauled on to the pavement as Meg slammed the door shut behind me.

Apparently I was going to the pub after all.

"OK, I'm not sure it's a good idea to do this now," I said, as I hurried after her. Meg strode on, her long legs eating up the pavement, not even pausing for me to catch up. She had to be freezing. Unless her anger was keeping her warm. "I mean, it's New Year's Eve. Sean's probably plastered already."

"Even better," she said shortly. "He won't ask too many questions."

"I'm pretty sure he'll ask some, though. What am I going to tell him?"

Meg rolled her eyes at me. "Haven't you figured out a story yet? Honestly, I knew I should have asked Becca to do this part."

"Becca's already doing everything else," I pointed out. "Which is quite a lot for someone who isn't actually getting married."

"Shh! The last thing we need is someone overhearing."

I stopped walking and waited for her to do the same. Just a few weeks ago she'd been the one joking about it loudly at my house. Now she was paranoid. What had changed?

"Are you coming?" Meg called from a few metres ahead.

"Not until you tell me what's got you so worked up tonight."

She huffed, loud enough for me to hear even at a distance, and stopped. "Let's just say my parents have upped their game," she said without turning round.

Well, that would explain the mood.

"What did they do?" I took a few steps towards her and she started walking again. Apparently I was going to be playing catch-up all night.

"It doesn't matter." She shook her head. "In five days any issues they have will be completely beside the point."

Five days. It was so damn close now.

"Well, if you want to talk about it—"

"I don't."

"Right."

Meg sighed and turned back to face me. "Look. I just want to get to this party, find Sean, get him to agree to lend us the car, then celebrate with a drink. Or two.

After all, in –" she glanced down at her watch – "three and a half hours, I'll be able to say that I'm getting married this year."

She flashed a grin at me then turned round again, picking up the pace even more, striding towards the town centre and leaving me no choice but to follow.

The pub Sean had chosen for ringing in the new year wasn't one I'd been to often; until a few months ago The Mermaid had been another run-down locals-only sort of a place with an older crowd, tucked away at the edge of town. One of Sean's classmates from school had taken it over recently and was trying to turn it into the new place for local twenty-somethings and students like Sean and his mates who were home for the holidays to go to. Apparently he figured that painting it a really unattractive lime green and commissioning a mural of an almost-topless mermaid on one wall would do it. Megan seemed to like it well enough, though, and she was in good company. The minute we were through the door, I lost sight of her in the crowd, even as I heard someone calling her name. Apparently she was here for the booze and I was here to do a job. Which started with finding my brother.

In the end, that was easier than I expected. I just headed towards the topless mermaid and found him sitting at an overcrowded table with a load of his mates – and Becca. Proving once and for all, I decided, that this wasn't just a bit of fun. Sean never invited girls on his guys' nights out. This was definitely something new, even if he wasn't admitting it yet.

"El! You made it!" Sean lifted his pint glass in greeting, sloshing some of the liquid over the side. "You got a drink?"

I shook my head. "Not yet. I'll brave the bar in a minute." At least since I'd turned eighteen at the start of the school year, I didn't have to worry about the potential embarrassment of not getting served any more. I couldn't imagine that Meg would have a problem – girls always got served younger than blokes in our town.

Sean manoeuvred his way out of his seat to reach me, making conversation easier as we didn't have to shout. Becca slid into his empty chair, already chatting with one of the other guys there.

"What changed your mind?" Sean asked.

"Did you know Mum was going out tonight?" I asked. Sean shrugged and shook his head. "Yeah. New bloke, apparently."

"Good for her!" Sean said with a grin. "No one should be alone on New Year's Eve. Not even idiot baby brothers." He tried to grab me in a head lock, apparently forgetting that I was now half a head taller than him and at least a couple of pints soberer.

I ducked out of the way. "Since you're in such a good mood … I have a favour to ask."

"Really?" Sean raised his eyebrows and waited. Behind him, I saw Becca turn just slightly towards us, obviously tuning into our conversation. She, of course, knew exactly what I was about to ask. "So? What's the favour?"

"I need to borrow your car. Next week. For a couple of days." The words came out in a bit of a rush and Sean got that irritating, knowing look on his face.

"Do you, now? And what, exactly, are you doing that needs my car?" Sean's smile somehow managed to be both patronizing and amused. "This wouldn't have anything to do with a girl, would it?" Half the guys around the table were obviously listening in now and one gave a little wolf whistle to prove it.

"Maybe," I said through gritted teeth. Where was Megan? She was the one making me do this in public. The least she could do was support me while I humiliated myself.

"Who? Oh God, not Crazy Amy again?" Sean said. "No, it won't be her because you guys split up, right? Actually, I think I saw her earlier – you'd better watch out.

She looks the sort to take revenge if she finds out you're planning some road trip with another girl."

"It's not Amy," I reassured him, ignoring the rest of his statement. "Look, I can't really go into details. But I need the car from next Wednesday. I'll be back before the weekend."

"Is it Megan?" Sean's face lit up at the idea. "It is, isn't it? It's Megan Hughes. Well, well, well…"

"It's not what you think," I said flatly.

Sean studied me long and hard, which would have been more intimidating if he wasn't wobbling slightly. Becca, meanwhile, got to her feet and disappeared in the direction of the bar. I watched her, wishing I could walk away just like that.

"OK," Sean said. "But only because you're my brother, and it's my duty to help you move on from Crazy Amy and get laid by some other girl, and fast. And if there's the slightest scratch or dent…"

"You mean other than the hundred or so it already has?" Sean's car was hardly a piece of art. It was hardly a car.

"Exactly." Sean clapped me on the shoulder. "I'm glad we understand each other."

I was just relieved that he was too drunk to ask any other questions.

"But remember," Sean said, as I turned to head for the

bar, a drink and Megan, in that order. "Don't do anything that I would do!"

The whole table fell about laughing and I smiled. "Oh, I think I'm pretty safe on that one," I told him.

I really couldn't see Sean eloping to Gretna Green for a marriage that wouldn't even get him laid.

Megan

It's easy enough to get served in our local pubs, even underage, as long as you don't get into trouble too often. I'd always managed to walk the fine line between having fun but not too much, so the barman handed over my vodka happily enough.

Once I'd thought I'd be pestering Lizzie to buy me my first drinks, as soon as she was old enough to get served. But she'd never really hung out in the pubs anyway. What had she been doing out on a boat with a load of drunk guys that night? It was totally not like Lizzie.

I couldn't help but wonder, over a year later, what had made that night different. And my conversation with Elliott on Christmas Eve hadn't really given me any answers at all – although it had left me with the impression that he might have some, if I could only ask the right questions.

I shook the thought away. Not tonight. I'd have the long drive up to Gretna Green to quiz him. Tonight, I had plans: make Elliott get us a car and get drunk. Simple as that.

As I made my way back through the crowd, looking for Becca, I started to relax a little. There was a band playing at the far end of the pub, down by where the pool tables usually were, and the music pounded around the building, over the heads of the people flooding into the place. Apparently The Mermaid was now *the* place to be on New Year's Eve. Who knew?

"Elliott's asking Sean about borrowing the car." Becca popped up beside me, drink in hand. Becca had been able to get served in the local pubs since she was fourteen, something every other girl in school had been jealous of. "Did you know he hadn't done that yet?"

"I just found out tonight." I supposed I should go and support him, really. After all, he was doing it for me. "Where are they?"

"At the back, by the ridiculous topless mural. When I left, Sean was guessing that Elliott wanted to borrow the car to go somewhere with you."

"Of course he was." How was it that we could make all these plans, put everything in place, lie to our parents and the first hint anyone got of something going on was because Elliott couldn't even ask his brother to borrow the car without giving everything away? I started towards them but Becca caught my arm, almost spilling my drink.

"Let's go over here." She pointed to an equally crowded corner of the bar, closer to the band. "We can talk."

Talk with my best friend or save Elliott from a difficult conversation with his brother?

Elliott could look after himself.

"If you want to talk, let's try outside," I suggested, as the band broke into another guitar-heavy song. Becca pulled a face but followed me into the frosty beer garden.

Outside wasn't much less packed than inside despite the chill, but it was noticeably quieter. Wrapping our arms round ourselves for warmth and getting as close to the outdoor heaters as we could manage, Becca and I perched on the edge of a damp picnic table, balancing our drinks on our knees.

"So? What's up?" I figured that if Becca wanted a proper talk on New Year's Eve, it had to be one of two things: a last-minute conversation to check I was absolutely certain I wanted to elope with Elliott, or a one-sided chat about Sean. Mentally I set up my own drinking game to go with the conversation. One sip every time Becca said the words Sean, Elliott, Gretna, elope or insane. Two if she suggested talking to my parents. And if she mentioned waiting for true love, I was downing the whole glass.

"It's Sean," Becca said. I took a sip.

"Of course it is. So, what's the deal with you two? Are you, what, dating?" Why did that sound so weird? God, did that mean we'd have to go on double dates when Elliott and I were married? Even if only one half of us would *actually* be in a relationship?

Becca snorted. It was surprisingly un-Becca-like. "No. *Definitely* not dating. Trust me, we're not going to be following you and Elliott up to Gretna to elope or anything."

Elliott, Gretna *and* elope. I took three quick sips. "Then what *are* you doing?"

"That's the problem." Becca's shoulders drooped as she stared into her glass. "I have absolutely no idea."

OK, maybe this wasn't a drinking-game conversation after all. I put my glass down and shuffled a little closer. "Well, what have you done so far? I mean, as a not-couple. Not, like, the graphic details or anything." I sighed. Apparently I was out of practice at this. "I mean, have you talked about your relationship at all?"

"I wouldn't even call it a relationship. More friends

with benefits," Becca admitted. "Mostly we're just…"

"Having sex?"

Becca blushed. "Not *only* that."

"So, what? What *are* you doing? I mean, you've only actually seen him a handful of times since the summer. What do you do the rest of the time?"

"Send text messages," Becca said glumly. "When we IM or text each other … we talk about everything, things I never thought about discussing with a guy. And when we do that, I feel *important* to him somehow. Like it's more than just the sex and having someone to talk to. But then he visits and … I don't know. I want to think he's coming here to see me, but then he stands me up or he's out with his friends. Even tonight … when he invited me to come out for New Year's Eve, I thought that meant something. But he's barely said two words to me all night."

"Which is better? The messages or the sex?" I reached for my glass. I needed a little help if I had to imagine Becca and Sean in bed. Becca blushed, the red in her cheeks nothing to do with the heaters overhead. "The sex, then."

"Honestly? They're both pretty fantastic. But—" She gave a pointed look around us to remind me we weren't exactly having this conversation in private.

In fact, when I checked, I realized there were at least three people listening in.

"You can tell me later," I agreed. "OK, well, I guess the question is: what do you *want* your relationship to be? Do you want to be his girlfriend? Or are you happy with a casual thing?" I had a feeling things would go a *lot* better if Becca wanted casual. Sean was kind of known for non-serious hook-ups, not long-term romance.

Becca gave a heavy sigh. "I guess I just … I want to know where I stand, is all. I mean, he's away at uni. I'll be going in September, hopefully. I'm not really thinking that this is forever or anything. I just wish I knew how he actually felt – if he feels anything at all. Does that make sense?"

"That makes perfect sense." I wrapped an arm round her shoulder. "And he's an idiot not to let you know."

"So what do I do?"

"Well, if it was me … I'd get up, finish my drink, go inside and dance to the band. Maybe flirt with the cute guitarist or something. And basically leave him to it until he's ready to come and talk to you in public and let you know where you stand."

"That actually sounds kind of fun." Becca grinned. "As long as you're planning on dancing with me."

"Of course!" I jumped down from the picnic table and held out a hand to pull Becca down, too. "But no flirting for me. I'm an engaged woman, don't you know?"

New message

To: Becca Maddox

Hey, any idea what my little bro wants my car for this week? He said it had something to do with a girl – not Crazy Amy, thank God. So, spill. You've been spending time with him and Meg lately. What's going on? Is my baby brother in lurve or what?

Becca is offline.

Elliott

The thing about New Year's Eve is that people have expectations. I mean, it's supposed to be the biggest night out of the year, right? Except we were still just in the same old pub in town. Although once I'd got asking Sean about the car out of the way, I have to admit, I had fun. It was kind of nice hanging out with my brother and catching up with some of his friends who used to be round our house all the time. I didn't see much of Megan, but when Sean came back from the bar he reported that she and Becca were dancing to the band, so I figured everything was OK there.

In fact, everything seemed fine until Amy showed up.

"Elliott?" I looked up from my pint to find her standing beside me, her eyes slightly unfocused. Her hair had come loose from its pins and her lipstick had worn away. I'd only seen Amy drunk a few times but she looked well on her way past tipsy right then. Behind her, Sean was making the sign of the cross with his fingers, which was *not* helpful. "I didn't expect to see you here. I know you usually spend New Year with your mum…"

"She went out. Had a date." I really didn't want to get drawn into a discussion about it with Amy. But already her eyes had widened and she'd slid on to the bench seat beside me.

"Are you OK with that? Because if you wanted to talk…"

"I'm fine," I said quickly, lifting my drink to my lips as if to prove it.

Amy looked disapprovingly at my pint which, given her obvious tipsiness, was pretty hypocritical of her. "Elliott, if you're upset—"

"I'm not."

"Still, drinking isn't the answer."

I gave her a long look until she had the grace to blush, just a little.

"I'm just saying, I'm here if you need me."

"I don't."

Amy jerked her head back at that, like I'd hurt her, and I swore. "I didn't mean… Look, I just mean I'm OK. That's all. Don't you need to get back to the others?" Because if there was anything more awkward than having a conversation with your drunk ex on New Year's

Eve while your brother pulled faces behind her back, I hadn't found it yet.

Amy glanced over her shoulder at the group of girls by the window who were watching us – and possibly Sean. Sean, fortunately, managed to stop his antics before Amy spotted him, and wandered back off to the bar again.

"I could," Amy said slowly, "but it's nearly midnight."

"Um, yeah? It is?"

What was I missing? I let the question hang there, but as I watched her eyes darken slightly I realized *exactly* what her point was, even before she said, "Don't you think we deserve a New Year's Eve kiss?"

"Amy ... we split up," I reminded her.

"I know. And we've been really good about it." She shifted just a little closer, her thigh pressed up against mine. She was wearing a short black dress over thick black tights, her bare arms and cleavage milk-white against the dark fabric. I knew that dress. I'd told her I liked her in that dress. "I know we've decided that a future together is too complicated right now..."

Had we? Was that what had happened between us?

"But it's New Year's Eve. No one should be alone at New Year."

"I don't think that's a very good idea," I said, sliding

along the bench seat away from her. "We need a clean break. For the new year."

Amy's face fell, just for a moment, then got stormy. "You should know what people are saying about you."

"Why should I care?" I asked, but she ignored me.

"They're saying that you're hot for Megan Hughes. That you're going to drag her down with you."

"Because I'm so low, right?" The anger built up in my chest. "I can only bring people down, just like my dad. So what, you believe that now, too?"

"I didn't say that." Amy dipped her head, avoiding my eyes.

"But you're thinking it."

"Well, you're the one who swore blind there was nothing going on with you and Megan," she shot back.

"There isn't," I snapped, standing up. "But that shouldn't make a damn bit of difference to you any more."

"Of course it does." She tried to tug me back down but I shook her off.

Then, across the bar, something else caught my attention and I stopped thinking about Amy at all.

The band were still playing as we approached midnight and the dancing had spilled out into the main part of the pub. In the middle of it all, I spotted Megan bobbing along in time to the music. Then some guy pushed up against her, his hands round her waist, and she stopped dancing. I leaned a little to the left, trying to get a clear sightline through the crowd to figure out what was happening, but it was too busy. Frowning, I stepped away from Amy.

"Where are you going?" Amy demanded, following me across the pub.

I didn't answer. I was too busy watching as Megan tried to pull away from the guy – except he wouldn't let go.

"Oh, I see. *Of course* there's nothing going on between you two. I must be stupid for thinking there was."

She sounded mad. Fine. I didn't care about that.

I cared about getting Megan away from that bastard.

I pushed my way through the crowd to reach Meg at the same time as she broke free of his grasp, spun round and punched him in the face. Any other girl would have slapped, or screamed, but not Meg. She went straight for the punch. That was one of the things I liked most about her – she didn't need me to save her.

But since the guy was now holding his bleeding nose, I decided it was probably best to get her out of there.

Fast.

Megan

They say that alcohol inhibits your decision-making processes but, truth be told, I'd have probably punched the guy even if I'd been stone-cold sober. Any man who doesn't let go and move away when I tell him to is asking for it. But he was the sort who couldn't stand being bested by a girl and he was a lot drunker than I was, anyway. So when Elliott swooped in, grabbed my arm and dragged me out of there, I decided to let him.

It was kind of nice to have someone looking out for me without trying to make all the decisions for myself for a change.

"You want to go back in, when things have calmed down?" he asked, once we were safely in the beer garden, and the pub door had swung shut behind us. "Or do you want to head home?"

I leaned against the wall and thought about it. My head was starting to feel a little bit buzzy around the edges, so it was probably time to leave. Before I did something stupid like punch some guy three times my size.

Oh, wait…

My hand throbbed but at least it wasn't bleeding or broken. Probably.

"Let's go," I said. "Becca had to leave anyway, so she won't be missing me. But … not straight home. I need some air first." And a bit of distance between pub-Megan and home-with-parents-Megan never went amiss, either. I could almost hear their horrified responses in my head. *Lizzie never got into fights…*

"We could walk along the beach?" Elliott suggested, and I smiled.

"You have the best ideas." Linking my non-throbbing hand through his arm, I let him lead me out of the beer garden, back on to the main road.

I don't know if Elliott noticed Amy looking out of the pub window, but she definitely saw us. For someone who'd broken up with him, she seemed awfully possessive still. With my sore hand, I gave her a small wave, hoping to convey 'just friends' vibes. She scowled.

The beach was cold and windy and damp − perfect. The chilly breeze blew away the cobwebs from my mind and the fresh sea air filled my lungs, wiping out the memories of the evening.

At least until Elliott said, "You want to tell me what happened with your parents tonight?"

I sighed. He deserved to know; after all, this was his business, too. Of course in five days, if everything went to plan, my parents would have no power over me *or* the flat. But still.

"My parents had an offer from a developer on Grandma Alice's flat." Elliott stopped walking as I spoke, so I did, too, turning to face him. "It was a really good offer, apparently."

"But it's your flat. They can't sell it without your permission, right?" There was no sign of panic in Elliott's voice but his face was blank – the way I'd noticed it always was when he was trying to hide what he was feeling. Which meant he *was* worried. It was nice to think I was getting better at reading this new Elliott.

"Right now? Technically, yes. But in five days, not a chance. And the developer doesn't need an answer for two weeks," I explained. "They've agreed to give me time to think about it."

"OK. OK. So as long as they don't just go ahead and sell the flat anyway in the next five days..."

"We're in the clear," I reassured him. "And anyway, if they did, the money would be mine as soon as we have that marriage certificate. We'd have to find somewhere else to live but we'd have the money to do that. Don't worry."

Elliott gave a short laugh that almost got lost in the wind. "This is so crazy. You know that, right? We're standing here talking about getting married, buying a flat, moving in together … and we're not even a couple. We've never even kissed. Amy wanted to kiss me at midnight and I said no because it felt weird. Because I'm getting married in five days, even though it's the most insane thing I've ever done."

We've never kissed… He was right. And somehow, that felt wrong.

I hadn't got into this for romance, or emotions – only escape. But standing there on the beach, looking up at his newly familiar face in the moonlight, I realized. *I want Elliott to kiss me. I want to kiss Elliott.*

But I couldn't. Because that wasn't our deal. And given that he was already freaking out, I couldn't risk doing anything that might spook him enough to make him back out. I had to stick to the plan.

His words echoed in my head. *The most insane thing I've ever done.* "So, what? You're having second thoughts?"

"Are you kidding?" Elliott laughed again, lighter this time, the sound whisked away by the wind. "I'm finally believing that we can do this. That we can move to London together. That I can go to UCL, have my dream career. I just … I don't want anything to get in the way of it now."

I knew that feeling. I smiled at him, the tension in my muscles finally releasing.

"It won't. We won't let it." I reached out and took his hand, squeezing it tightly. He did the same back to me and, as I looked up into his eyes, I knew that this was it. *This* was the moment of no return. Everything leading up to this second had just been an idea, a fantasy. Now we were here and it was real and it was going to happen. The next five days were all downhill from this point.

We were getting married.

And suddenly, I was weirdly excited.

Elliott

"We missed midnight," Megan said, checking her watch as we reached her house. Above us, the moon was big and round, just past full, and its light shone down and made her hair almost white.

"It's probably for the best," I said. Midnight at the pub could have been messy. Although part of me was a little sad that we'd missed the moment the clock ticked over into the new year. It must have been while we were on the beach together. We could have celebrated... No. I wasn't having those thoughts. "How's your hand?" I asked, changing the subject quickly.

Meg flexed her fingers and looked down at her reddened knuckles. "Throbbing."

"Put some ice on it when you get inside. Once the swelling goes down it'll hurt less."

The corners of Meg's lips turned up into a smile. "Speaking from experience?"

"Yes. Sean's, mostly."

"He got into a lot of fights when he was younger, didn't he? After … after your dad left," she said tentatively.

"Yeah." I shoved my hands in my pockets and looked away. She already knew the story as well as anyone else in town and I didn't want to talk about it.

"It wasn't fair, what people said."

"You mean what they still say." Bitterness. The sort of acidy, unfair feeling that meant I just couldn't let it drop. That was why I had to get out of St Evaline. I didn't want to end up with nothing of me left except my anger.

"They shouldn't." She rested her sore hand against my arm and it felt like a static shock. "You're not your dad."

"I know that."

"And I'm just saying, so do I. I always have."

I looked over and met her gaze. For the longest time, I'd thought that my mum and Sean were the only people who knew that. And then Amy.

But Megan knew it. Megan knew *me*.

She dipped her head and broke our staring contest. "So, Sean agreed to lend us the car?"

"He did. God knows why, since I couldn't even tell him what I wanted it for."

Megan shrugged, dropping her hand away from my arm. "He's your brother. He trusts you."

"With his life, sure. With his car..." I shook my head. "My brother is a mystery to me." It was weird, having someone in your life that you knew so well but didn't understand at all. But then, Megan was a bit like that, too.

"So you don't know what he's doing with Becca, either?" she asked.

"I don't think *Sean* knows what's going on there."

Meg sighed, leaning against the front door. "That makes two of them, then." She grinned up at me. "At least we know exactly what sort of a relationship we're getting into."

"We do." We even had it in writing, thanks to Becca. A detailed plan for our marriage and what we each got out of it. I was sure it wasn't legal but it was good enough for us. We knew where we stood. As long as her parents didn't sell the flat in the next five days...

I shook the thought away. I couldn't worry about that.

"Thanks for tonight," Meg said softly.

"You seemed to be holding your own," I pointed out. "It's not like you really *needed* me there."

"No. But it's nice to have someone on your side, sometimes." She smiled at me and reached up on tiptoes to press a soft kiss to the corner of my mouth, so close I couldn't tell if she was aiming for my cheek or my lips.

If her touch had been static, this was a full-blown

electric shock. My face tingled where her lips touched my skin and I wanted more than anything to kiss her properly.

But I couldn't. Megan was my future, my way out of St Evaline. She couldn't be anything else. I needed her too much to risk that.

"Happy New Year, Elliott," she said, stepping back. With one last smile, she slipped inside, the door swinging shut behind her.

SEAN
Hey. Since you're ignoring my IM, I thought I'd text... Happy New Year.

BECCA
You, too.

SEAN
Shame you didn't stick around for a kiss at midnight...

BECCA
My mum called. The babysitter got sick and I had to head home to take over.

BECCA
And honestly? I didn't think you'd notice.

SEAN
I notice everything.

BECCA
Yeah? How long did it take you to notice I'd even gone?

SEAN
I noticed the guy you were dancing with.

BECCA
He was cute. And none of your business.

SEAN
I guess not. But I guess ... maybe I'd like it to be?

Megan

"Do you want a lift to college with that?" Dad asked from the kitchen doorway, as I struggled to settle my oversized rucksack full of hiking gear and waterproofs on to my shoulders. For a cover story, our hiking trip in the Brecons required a lot of props.

"I'm fine." I flashed him a smile to convince him. Since we weren't actually meeting at the college, a lift there would make things considerably *more* difficult. "This trip is all about individual survival techniques. Guess I'd better start with being able to carry my own bags!"

Dad laughed and saluted me with his cup of coffee. "Well, have a great trip, then. We'll see you the day after tomorrow, right?"

I nodded. "Right." The day after tomorrow, I'd be a married woman. I'd be in control of my own life for the first time in seventeen years.

And I'd probably be in a hell of a lot of trouble with my parents. But that was a problem for Future Meg. Right now I was just focused on meeting Elliott and getting on the road. One step at a time, that was the way to handle this.

Anything else was just too overwhelming.

Like thinking about New Year's Eve, and the almost-kiss I gave Elliott, right after I promised myself I wouldn't. I was just hoping he'd chalk it up to drunkenness and forget it. Something I'd been totally unable to do over the last few days.

But I couldn't waste time worrying about it now. I had a wedding to get to.

"I'll see you, then. Bye, Dad!" I slammed the front door behind me. This was it. My chance to break free and choose my own future.

But first I had to carry this damn rucksack all the way to Oracle, where Becca was waiting to swap out my waterproofs for a wedding dress and my maps for a file of paperwork for the marriage.

The bells over the door sounded like wedding bells as I entered the shop and Becca started humming 'Here Comes The Bride' the minute she saw me.

"More like 'Get Me to the Church on Time'," I joked, singing a few snatches as I put down my bag.

"Where's Elliott?"

"He'll be here," Becca said, perfectly calm. Reaching behind the counter, she pulled out the bag containing my dress and shoes and a plastic folder full of paperwork. "Although I should warn you, Sean was asking a lot of questions about what Elliott wanted the car for. He even IMd me to ask if it was about you."

I froze. "What did you say?" If this all fell apart because of Sean's suspicions, I would be so mad...

"Nothing, of course." Becca sounded mildly offended.

"Sorry. I just really don't want anything to go wrong now, when we're so close."

"I know." Becca tilted her head as she looked at me. "So, you're definitely going through with this?"

I stared at her in amazement. "What, did you think we were just playing around for the entire last month and a half?"

"No," she said slowly. "I guess I just thought you might have ... changed your mind, before we got this far."

"Come to her senses, you mean," Elliott's voice rang out from the door. "Fortunately for me, she doesn't have that many." He flashed me a grin to show he was joking and I pulled a face back at him, ignoring the way my heart beat a little faster at his smile. Apparently we were ignoring the kiss. Perfect.

"I thought you might come to your senses, too," Becca said, studying Elliott.

"No such luck. In fact, most people would tell you I have even less sense than her." Elliott held out a hand for the bags and I gave them to him, taking care to make sure our hands didn't touch. "I'll get these stashed in the boot."

"No trouble getting the car from Sean?" I asked.

Elliott shrugged the rucksack on to one shoulder, shaking his hair out of his eyes, and I focused on his hand resting on the strap of the bag. *Looking* at hands was safe, right? Except watching Elliott's made me think about him touching me...

"Why would there be?" he asked, and I struggled to remember the question I'd posed. The car. Right.

As he disappeared out of the door to load up the car, Becca leaned close to me and whispered, "You're absolutely sure about this? That you know what you're doing, I mean?"

"Of course I am! We've spent long enough planning it."

Becca shook her head. "That's not what I mean. Are you sure you know what you're doing with Elliott?"

"Marrying him," I said, very slowly. "Just like we planned."

"Yes, but is that all?" How did she know? I swear, sometimes I thought that working at Oracle gave Becca psychic powers.

The memory of a tiny midnight kiss filled my brain all over again. It had been nothing – just a friendly peck on the cheek. Barely even that.

Except it had been the first thing I remembered when I woke up on January first – until my knuckles started throbbing and I remembered the incident on the dance floor. But it was still the only thing I could think about when I looked at him. Which was crazy. It wasn't even a proper kiss.

Elliott was a friend. And, right now, a means to an end.

"I know what I'm doing," I told Becca, filling my voice with all the confidence I didn't quite feel. "Don't worry."

Elliott appeared in the doorway again, car keys in hand, and I made myself look at him as just a friend. A boy I'd known my whole life. Nothing more. "Ready?"

"Ready." I held the folder of paperwork close to my chest. "See you in a couple of days," I said, turning to Becca.

"Good luck," she said. "Stay in touch, let me know how it's going."

"Will do. And you'll cover for us at this end, if anything comes up?" The plan. That was what mattered here.

Becca nodded. "Of course. And … have a brilliant wedding!"

Elliott

I tried not to let my nerves show as we pulled out of town but my hand kept tapping against the wheel on the straight roads and I had to wipe my sweaty palms on my jeans more than once, so Megan probably suspected. She didn't say anything, though, which I appreciated. Maybe the nerves were even getting to her finally.

I wasn't used to being afraid, not like this. People talking about me, lads wanting to beat me up, rough seas … they were nothing. I knew how to handle them.

But this … this was completely unknown. For all of Becca's spreadsheets and plans, I just didn't know how to imagine what came next. And that was terrifying.

We drove in silence, punctuated only by the robotic voice of Megan's phone issuing directions. The route we'd chosen took us straight past where we were supposed to be hiking that week – the Brecon Beacons. As we passed a sign, Megan snapped a photo with the camera round her neck, then suddenly turned her attention from the scenery back to me.

"So have you seen Amy since New Year?" she asked, and I wished she'd go back to staring at the sheep. I really didn't want to talk about Amy. Or New Year, for that matter.

"No." I knew I should leave it there. I didn't want to encourage her. And yet, I couldn't help but ask, "Why?"

"You know she was watching us. When we left the pub together." She glanced back out of the window as she said the last part. I wondered if she was remembering the same thing I was – that weird, not-quite-just-friends-but-not-quite-anything-else kiss.

That kiss I hadn't been able to get out of my head ever since – even though I knew I had to.

"I was with her when you threw that punch," I explained. "She saw what happened. She knew why we were leaving together." She might not have liked it but she knew why. And it was none of her business any more, anyway.

"And she didn't mind?" Meg's gaze was fixed on my face again. I kept my eyes on the road and tried to ignore the way it made me feel. "I mean, you said she was hanging around waiting for a midnight kiss…" She broke off suddenly and I knew what she was thinking.

"I wasn't going to kiss her. We've split up, remember.

Look, can we stop talking about my ex-girlfriend? I mean, we're getting married tomorrow. It's kind of inappropriate." I tried to make it sound like a joke but Meg didn't laugh. When I risked a glance over, her eyebrows were raised so high they'd disappeared under her fringe.

"Maybe if this was a *real* wedding," she said finally. "But El, we're going to be living together when we get to London. We'll basically be the only people we know in the whole city, at least to start with. We're friends, right? And friends talk about this stuff."

"Do they have to?" I'd *never* talked to my friends about this stuff. I'd barely talked to my *girlfriend* about this stuff.

Megan shifted round in her seat so one foot was folded up underneath her and she was facing me. "Maybe we should talk about *this*."

"This? What this?" The road started to twist a little more as we left the last village for miles and weaved our way through the foothills. I made an extra effort to focus all my attention on where we were going, rather than wherever Megan was taking the conversation.

"How it will be between us when we're in London." At her words, my mind dived away from the road and into a different world. One where Megan and I were married, living together ... and anything but 'just friends'.

I bit the inside of my cheek, hoping the pain would force the image away. The last thing I needed to be imagining was Megan and I together. We had a deal, an agreement.

"Becca's already planned all that out for us, hasn't she?" There were spreadsheets. Spreadsheets were possibly the least sexy thing in the world.

"The financial side, sure. Even the divorce. But you know Becca – she focuses on the stuff you can make lists about – not the stuff you have to live."

"How do you mean?" I asked, frowning at the road ahead.

Megan gave a frustrated sigh. She hated explaining herself, I remembered suddenly. She wanted everyone to instantly get her ideas the way she did – a flash of impulse and imagination. But not everyone's brains worked that way.

"I mean ... I want us to be more than just flatmates or for you to just be my lodger. I want us to be friends. So maybe we need some ground rules for living together – like, do we want to cook together or have separate shelves in the fridge? Will we split the chores or just look after our own stuff? What do we do if one of us wants to bring a date home? That kind of thing."

A date. The rest of her list flew straight out of the

window and I focused in on that last point.

I would be living with Megan in London and she would be dating. Or I might be dating. And she would bring home these guys and I'd have to pretend to like them or be friends with them. And I'd have to explain to every girl I met that my incredibly beautiful flatmate was just a friend and sound like I believed it.

What happened if one of us fell in love? Being married to someone else was the sort of complication that was hard to explain.

Suddenly, I realized there was a whole side to this plan I hadn't given anywhere near enough thought to.

And if I hadn't thought about this, what else had I missed? A rising sensation of panic began bubbling up inside me. I'd always known this plan was crazy, but was it *stupid* as well? I needed a sign. Something to show me I was doing the right thing.

Something other than a sheep wandering out into the winding mountain road as I drove, preferably.

"Um, you're right. We should probably talk about—" Swearing loudly, I swerved to miss the sheep, the right-hand wheels rising up over the rough grass at the side of the road. Praying we hadn't hit any rocks and punctured a tyre, I steered us back on to the narrow road that made its way up and around the mountain. I shifted down a gear as a sharp bend approached, gripping the wheel more firmly. Thank God the car kept moving smoothly and my heart rate started to slow again. "But maybe later. When I'm not driving."

"Sure," Meg said, swivelling round to sit properly in her seat again. "Sorry."

"That's OK."

"It's just, I was thinking—"

A loud, crunching noise interrupted her as something in the underbelly of the car gave way and we rolled to a stop.

Perfect.

I pulled on the handbrake and rested my head on the steering wheel. We hadn't even managed to leave Wales and everything was already falling apart.

Hadn't I asked for a sign?

Megan

"What's wrong with the car?" I asked, picking nervously at a loose thread in my jeans. *This* was not the plan.

"It's a sign," Elliott muttered from where his forehead was resting against the steering wheel. "A sign that we are insane and should go home."

"No." That was simply not an option. Not when we'd come this far. "Look, we just need to get someone out to fix the car. Or something." Like I knew anything about what you did with cars that didn't work. My dad upgraded his every few years and looked after it like it was made of rubies. Mum left all her car stuff to Dad, so hers was basically treated like emeralds. They never kept one long enough for it to actually break down.

On the side of a mountain. In the middle of nowhere. While trying to elope.

It occurred to me that one thing I could learn a lot

about from my parents was the importance of making sure that *somebody* took care of the car maintenance.

"We need to call Sean," Elliott said, lifting his head at last. Apparently his minor breakdown had only been temporary. I hoped the car's was as easily fixable.

"And tell him what?" I asked. "I mean, he's going to have a lot of questions."

"I know." Elliott unclipped his seat belt and turned towards me. "Look, Megan, maybe this *is* a sign."

"I never had you down for believing in that kind of thing."

"I don't," Elliott said. "But in this particular case, I might be willing to make an exception." He leaned a little further across the handbrake and grabbed my hand, pulling it away from the loose thread I was worrying. "Just ... think of this as our last chance to back out. Think about that massive list you just gave me of things we haven't talked about yet. What else haven't we thought of? Look, we could just call Sean, tell him we broke down, get someone out here to fix the car ... then head home with no one any the wiser. We'll say the hike was called off due to bad weather and Sean won't spill about the car as long as we sort it now. We could just forget all this."

My hand felt warm where he held it and I almost

asked him if that was really what he wanted. But I knew it wasn't. He didn't want to go back to St Evaline any more than I did. He was just scared.

When we were kids, this happened all the time. I'd come up with some crazy plan and Elliott would go along with it until the last moment, when he'd suddenly say that we should call it off. But he never meant it. He just needed me to be brave for both of us and push on through.

Strange to think that this new, bigger, bolder Elliott needed that, too.

I could still be brave.

"And forget moving to London? Living our own lives – the lives we actually want?" I shook my head as I reached for the door handle. "No, thanks. We're doing this."

Outside a light drizzle was falling, the sort that isn't proper rain but drenches you all the way through anyway. It felt icy cold on my skin. Behind me I heard Elliott sigh, then open his door and get out of the car.

"No reception," he said after a few moments, and when I turned round, he was holding his phone up to the sky, trying to get a signal.

I pulled my phone out of my pocket and checked. "Same. Damn, looks like we can't phone Sean."

"Or anybody else," Elliott pointed out.

I stared along the road leading up the mountain, then behind us at the path we'd already driven. OK. So, the plan was scuppered. That meant we needed a new one.

"When was the last time we saw another car?" I asked, still thinking.

"That village," Elliott said. "Just before the road started to climb." The village. Well, that was a plan right there, wasn't it?

"Do you remember the time we ran away from home when we were seven?" I asked.

"You mean when we got lost in the countryside and you made me carry all the bags?" Of course that was what he'd remember about the adventure. Not the jam sandwiches we ate by the side of the road or the epic game of I Spy we played.

"Well, this time we know where we're going." I grabbed my rucksack from the back seat and Elliott groaned as he figured out my plan. "And I promise to carry my own bag."

"You'd better," he grumbled.

"At least it's all downhill," I said reassuringly, settling my bag on to my back. "And we *did* tell our parents we were hiking."

Elliott

The village at the bottom of the hill wasn't huge, even by Welsh standards, but it had a pub, a shop and a bus stop, which Megan declared was all we could possibly need. How she was still in such good spirits after our two-mile walk in the drizzle, her hair damp and heavy around her face and that stupid rucksack on her back, was beyond me. She even paused to take some shots of the village with the mountains in the background.

"This place has the most fantastic views," she said, swinging round to take a photo of me scowling in front of the bus timetable.

I pulled my phone from the pocket of my waterproof coat. "It also has phone reception. Finally. I'm going to call Sean."

Meg rolled her eyes. "Fine. I'm going to go and figure out how we get to Gretna without a car. We can't sit around waiting for Sean's to get fixed." She crossed the road and wandered off in the direction of the pub. Given how the day had gone so far, I didn't have a great deal of faith in whatever the next plan would turn out to be.

I huddled underneath the bus shelter, dropped my bag on to the seat and called Sean.

"Hey. What's up? How's the romantic road trip going?" For a moment I panicked that Sean had figured out exactly what we were up to, before I realized that he was just guessing. He knew I had his car and that it was something to do with Megan. Romantic road trip was a pretty obvious guess. Typical Sean.

"So, about your car..." I started.

"Tell me you did not crash it." Sean was suddenly serious. "Tell me – and I want to hear these exact words – Sean, I did not crash your car."

"Sean, I did not crash your car," I parroted back to him. Sean sighed with relief. "But your car is a pile of junk that broke down halfway up a mountain." OK, hill.

"My car is not a— It broke down?"

"Yeah. It sort of went 'crunch' and stopped moving."

"Have you tried... No, you know nothing about cars. They are not the same as boats. Don't touch it."

"Not a problem." Especially since it was currently two miles away, up a hill.

The other end of the line went crackly, like Sean

had his hand over the microphone. I heard a muffled conversation going on but couldn't pick out the words. Then the line cleared.

"OK, so just stay by the car. Lucky for you, I'm with my mate Iain. He's a mechanic. If he can drive us out to where you are, he can fix it and I can drive it home and you can never go near it again. Sound good?"

"Um, sort of. Except there was no phone reception by the car. We had to walk two miles back to the last village we drove through."

"You left my car broken and alone on a mountain?" It didn't escape me that Sean clearly had considerably more concern for his car than his brother.

"So I could call you," I pointed out.

Sean sighed heavily. "OK, tell me exactly where you are. We're on our way."

Megan

The Red Dragon was a typical, middle-of-nowhere Welsh pub – the sort my Grandad Jones used to take me and Lizzie to when we went out for drives on Saturdays, before he died. Sometimes Elliott would tag along and we'd sit in the corner with soft drinks and a couple of bowls of chips, while the rain fell outside and Grandad nursed his pint at the bar with locals he'd befriend.

In fact, when I walked in, the first thing I clocked was the two old guys standing at the bar, talking to the woman behind it. Of course the minute I arrived they stopped talking and stared at me instead. I got the feeling they weren't used to strangers in there.

"Hi!" I said, smiling warmly. "Um, I wonder if you guys could help me. Our car broke down a couple of miles away and my fiancé is phoning for someone to come and pick it up now. But we really need to get to

Gretna Green before tomorrow…"

"Gretna Green, is it?" The guy with the bushy white moustache looked knowingly at his friend.

"Aren't you a little young to be getting married?" the landlady asked, looking me up and down.

I tried to look mature. "Not in Scotland," I told her.

"Hmm."

"The thing about marriage…" began the other guy, who was older, wearing a green hat and a navy jumper with holes in it over his beer belly. "I've always said this, even when my May was still alive. The thing that everyone gets wrong about marriage is—"

"It's not about finding the right person," white moustache man chorused along with him. "Bill, you've been saying that for twenty-five years and I still have no idea what you mean by it."

"And why am I not surprised it's taken you twenty-five years to ask, Jeffrey Tanner?" the landlady grumbled.

"Well, if you'd said yes when I proposed all those years ago, maybe I'd have had reason to ask sooner," Jeffrey said.

The landlady snorted in response. "Do you want a drink, love?" she added, turning to me.

"Just a Diet Coke, please. And maybe some crisps?"

While she fetched my drink, I boosted myself up on to the bar stool next to Bill. "So, what does it mean?"

"You're a bright girl," Bill said, smiling at me approvingly. "When I was your age, I thought I already knew everything."

"Well, I've never been married before," I pointed out. "I figure there's probably a lot still to learn there."

Bill lifted his pint to his mouth and took a long sip. Beside him, Jeffrey rolled his eyes and said, "Oh, you're in for it now, missy. Bill can talk for hours once you get him started. Especially after his first pint."

Shooting his friend a glare, Bill put down his glass. "What it means is, you can find the person you think is absolutely perfect – your Mr Right in this case," he said, nodding at me. "But it won't mean a damn thing if *you're* not the right person."

I frowned. "The right person for him, you mean?"

"The right person for *you*," Bill said. "You have to be *your* you, whoever that is, not the you you think you're supposed to be or the you you want to be, or even the you you think *they* want you to be. And you have to work at it. Marriage is hard work, missy, I hope you know that." He heaved himself off his stool. "And with that, I'm going to the bog."

The landlady snorted. "How romantic."

But I was still thinking about his words, trying to pick out the meaning between all the 'yous' and the 'theys'. "Do you think he's right? That for a marriage to work, you have to be yourself?" I thought back over the guys I'd dated and the sort of Megan they'd all wanted me to be. Dylan had wanted me to be the pretty blonde on his arm — and in his bed — even if I'd only realized it too late. But Elliott ... he just wanted me to be his way of affording university. And I could definitely be that.

"He's part right," the landlady said, after a moment. "There's no point going into marriage pretending about anything — it always comes out in the end, anyway. But as for being yourself ... that's not just advice for marriage. That's a rule for living, as far as I'm concerned."

She left my Coke and crisps on the bar and wandered off to wipe down some tables on the other side of the pub. Leaving me alone with Jeffrey of the bushy white moustache.

"So," he said, reaching for his pint. "You need to get to Gretna Green, eh? Well then, let's see what we can do about that. As long as those two haven't put you off."

I grinned. "No chance. So, what were you thinking?"

Elliott

By the time I'd hung up on Sean and popped into the village shop for supplies, the drizzle had turned into proper rain, belting down and bouncing off the road. Part of me was kind of glad I didn't have to drive through it – especially since every third drop that landed on my face as I ran across to the pub seemed to have ice in it.

"Elliott!" Meg's voice rang out the moment I stepped into the pub. I glanced around and found her sitting at the bar along with a couple of old guys – like, properly old. In their seventies, for sure.

"This is Mr Right, is it?" one of them asked.

"It certainly is," she said. "Good news!"

Was that a question? "Um, yeah, I guess? Sean and his mate Iain are driving up to fix the car, so they can give us a lift home. I'm never allowed to drive Sean's car again, but—"

"We're not going home," Meg interrupted. "We're

going to take the train. It'll take longer but I think we can just about make it." She waved her phone at me. "The nearest station is five miles away but Jeffrey here has very kindly offered us a lift. Isn't that nice?" She beamed at the slightly younger of the two guys and he grinned back under his bushy white moustache.

"Well, that's … will we get to Scotland in time?" I asked, all the problems with the plan suddenly surfacing again. There was a reason we'd planned to drive. The train – or rather, trains, as we'd have to change several times – took almost twice as long. "Do we have money for tickets? And what about Sean?"

"You text Sean, tell him where the car is – he's got the spare keys, right? Great. So just tell him we decided to catch the train instead. We'll still be home the day after tomorrow, it'll be fine." She gave Jeffrey's arm a friendly pat. "You just leave the rest to me and Jeffrey."

"We'll get you where you need to be, young man," Jeffrey said with a wink.

I gave him a lukewarm smile and sent a text to my brother.

Then I turned off my phone so he couldn't call and yell at me. Better safe than sorry and all that.

Megan insisted on taking photos of her new friends and the pub landlady before we left. And since the trains weren't very frequent, we had plenty of time.

"Now, remember what I told you," the older guy said as he patted Megan's hand. "Marriage isn't about finding the right person."

"I remember." Megan kissed him on the cheek. "And thank you."

"You stop back here and show us your wedding photos," the landlady added, leaning in for a hug.

"Definitely!" Megan promised.

"How do you do that?" I murmured to her, as we followed Jeffrey out of the pub and into the car park. "Make friends in seconds, wherever you go." I'd lived in St Evaline my whole life, near enough, and I could count my friends on one hand.

Lizzie had always resented that, I remembered, thinking of countless days on the beach when we were kids, when Megan had banded together with all the other children, leaving Lizzie and I working on our sandcastles alone.

Strange to think what opposites they'd been, even then.

But Megan just shrugged. "I like people," she said. "I guess that tends to make them like me."

Was it really as simple as that? "I guess I tend to expect people to be against me, until they prove otherwise."

"There you go, then," Megan said, just as Jeffrey came to a halt.

Right in front of a bloody tractor.

"Here we go!" he said, beaming proudly as he gestured to it. "Your wedding car awaits!"

Sean

Decline

Accept

Becca: Hello? Sean?

Sean: OK, seriously, you need to tell me what's going on.

Becca: You're calling me. Using the telephone. I know that's unusual for you, but really—

Sean: I mean with Elliott. He just called to say that the car has broken down halfway up a mountain—

Becca: Oh God, is he OK? Is Meg all right?

Sean: They're fine. Apparently, instead of waiting with the car like I told them to, they're off to catch a train to wherever it is they're going. He sent me a text. And now his phone is off. So you need to tell me where they're going. Right now.

Becca: Sean, stop it. Go and fetch your car and stop worrying about Elliott. He's a big boy now, you know.

Sean: He's my little brother. And I want to know where he is.

Becca: You know he's with Meg. Isn't that enough?

Sean: Ha! Trust me, that only makes it worse. Look, where are you? Are you at Oracle?

Becca: Yeah. Why?

Sean: I'm coming over. It's time you told me what the hell has been going on with my brother lately.

Megan

There aren't that many trains that go through stations in middle-of-nowhere Wales to take stranded teens to Scotland.

We'd missed the first train of the day and the next one was still over an hour away by the time Jeffrey dropped us at the station and drove off again. On his tractor. I purposefully hadn't mentioned that part to Elliott. I guessed – correctly, as it turned out – that he'd have a problem with it. Still, it got us there. Eventually. Which is more than you could say for Sean's car.

"This is a station?" Elliott asked, dropping his bag on to the platform.

"Apparently so," I said. I could understand his confusion. Apart from a few steps up to a stretch of concrete about the width of a pavement, and a small wooden bench with a flimsy plastic shelter, the only way you could tell that trains were actually supposed to stop there was the white wooden sign painted with the name of the nearest village. The same village we'd just been in – five miles away. Who put a station that far away, anyway?

"How long until the train?" Elliot settled himself on to the rickety-looking bench. I looked around wistfully, as if a nice, warm waiting room might suddenly appear if I wished hard enough.

I really, really wanted that waiting room.

"Another hour." I squeezed on to the bench next to him. I'd had enough of raindrops down my collar for one lifetime. Even my bra was soaked through.

I fished in my bag for the small microfibre towel I'd shoved in after a reminder text from Becca when I was packing the night before. As I pulled it out, something else came with it – a book I definitely hadn't packed. I caught it as it tumbled from the towel, saving it from the puddles at my feet. Then I grinned as I read the title.

"What's that?" Elliott asked.

"*Eloping with the Earl*," I said with relish. "This is the first romance I ever read – and where Becca and I learned about Gretna Green. Among other things. She must have shoved it in my bag while we were at Oracle." I flipped it open to the first page.

"You're going to read it? Now?"

"Why not? It's not like there's anything else to do. Besides, I'm trying to save my phone battery and I need a distraction." I ran the towel absently over my hair as I scanned the first few lines. Then, as I dried off my neck, I had a brilliant idea. "In fact, we can both enjoy it! I'll read it aloud."

Elliott groaned and slumped down on the bench, his head tipped back against the wood, his feet sticking out into the rain. But he didn't actually say no.

"Great! Chapter One..."

I got as far as the part where Lady Isabella meets Earl Raymond and promptly manages to insult him while also gaining the impression that he's a spy before my phone starting buzzing in my pocket.

"'Sir, I am certain that...' Oh, hang on." I'd assumed it would just be my parents again – I'd been ignoring their calls since before the car broke down, figuring they were just checking up on me like normal and that I could claim no signal in the hills – but when I checked the screen, it was Becca. "Hey, what's up?"

"OK, so don't lose it." Not entirely reassuring.

"Why would I lose it?"

"The college called your parents," Becca said. I could almost hear her wincing on the other end.

"What the hell? I thought you were going to call

in sick for me?"

"I did!" Becca protested. "Left a message with the secretary and everything."

"Then what was the problem?" Unless Becca had just been the least convincing fake parent of all time, that should have been the end of it.

"Apparently your *real* mum emailed your tutor about setting up a meeting – something about university applications, I think – and mentioned the hiking trip."

"The imaginary hiking trip."

"Exactly."

I sighed. "And to think I actually hiked down a mountain in the Brecons today and everything."

"Yeah, what's this about Sean's car breaking down?" Why wasn't I surprised that Sean had shared that news with her already? I filled her in quickly on the change of plan, before something else occurred to me.

"Hang on. How do you know the college called my parents?"

"Because your mum rang me," Becca said. "About two minutes after I got off the phone with Sean. Both of them wanted to know where you are."

"And what did you tell them?"

"That I had no idea. But I don't think either of them believed me."

Elliott was sitting up straight now, staring at me, waiting for an update. What to tell him? I didn't want him to revert to his maybe-we-should-just-go-home scheme, not when the train would be here in ten minutes.

I bit my lip and made a decision. "OK. Just stick to the story, right? As far as you know, we are hiking. We'll be on a train north in ten minutes and they'll never catch up with us then – especially if they don't know where we're headed. That's your job, OK?"

"Got it," Becca said. In the background I heard bells chime, signalling someone opening the door at Oracle. "Got to go. Sean's here."

"He's there? What are you going to—" I started, but she'd already hung up.

"Everything OK?" Elliott asked, looking suspicious.

I shrugged. "Mum found out we made up the hiking trip. That's all. Now, where were we? Oh, yeah. Chapter Three." I started to read again, but I got the impression Elliott wasn't really listening.

Even I was finding it hard to care about Lady Isabella's elopement. I was too concerned about my own.

Elliott

Finally the train rattled to a stop at the station – I'd been half afraid it might just storm on through, leaving us stranded. We were having that sort of a day. We jumped into the carriage and out of the rain with relief, figuring we'd buy our tickets on the train.

Except even though we were on the train and back on our way to Gretna, Megan was still reading that damn book. Thankfully, our coach was empty of other passengers. Before she started reading, we took it in turns to dry off and get changed in the tiny, smelly toilet cubicle. I was glad I'd brought spare clothes, as well as the smart trousers and shirt I'd packed to wear for the wedding itself. We spread our wet clothes out across the seats and hoped they'd dry enough for us to put them back in our bags by the time we reached Crewe, where we had to change for the next leg.

Eventually even Meg got sick of reading and lapsed

into silence across the table. When I checked again, she'd dozed off.

I set an alarm on my phone for five minutes before we were due into Crewe, leaned back and shut my eyes, too.

Crewe station was freezing cold, grey and full of flashing yellow signs showing delayed trains. Including ours.

"OK. Well, we had a decent connection time in Carlisle," Megan said, checking the train app. "So as long as it doesn't get any later, we should be fine."

"And if it does?"

"Then we'll catch the next one!" She nudged me with her backpack. "Don't be so negative. I'm going to go and check out the shops. I'll meet you in the waiting room."

The café by the waiting room had the usual assortment of soggy pasties and plastic-wrapped sandwiches, so I picked us up a couple of butties and some crisps to go with what was left of the biscuits I'd bought at the village shop earlier. I grabbed a couple of coffees, too, to try and warm us up.

Finding a table in the corner, I laid out our dinner and settled back against the worn fabric of the seat. My eyes already felt gritty from too much travelling, and my clothes smelled damp and musty. More than anything,

I wanted to get to our hotel in Gretna Green and take a shower.

Huh. Even a few hours ago, bumping along in Jeffrey's stupid tractor, my first thought would have been that I wanted to get home. But somehow, without even realizing it, I'd passed the point of no return. I couldn't imagine going back any longer. I only wanted to go forwards.

"What are you smiling at?" Megan dropped into the seat opposite me and reached for the chicken and sweetcorn sandwich. "Ooh, is this for me?"

"Help yourself," I said, pushing it towards her. "And nothing. Not really. Just ... can I borrow your phone a second?"

She looked instantly suspicious. "Who are you calling?"

"No one," I promised. "I just want to check something. And the internet on mine is rubbish."

Still looking sceptical, Megan handed over her phone.

"What's your passcode?" I asked, pressing the home button.

"One five zero five." I typed it in as she spoke the numbers, only realizing as the home screen opened what they meant.

"Lizzie's birthday." I looked up and caught her eye but she glanced away, tearing a chunk off her sandwich.

"Yeah. What are you doing, anyway?"

I let her change the subject and opened the maps app, tapping in our starting point and current location. "Checking our route so far." A hundred and seventy miles from St Evaline to Crewe. I deleted it, and typed in Crewe to Gretna Green. A hundred and fifty-four miles.

"We're over halfway," I said, handing the phone back.

"Past the point of no return, huh?" Megan grinned across the table at me as she said just what I'd been thinking.

"Exactly." There was no going back now. For either of us.

"All we need now is a train. And in the meantime..." She pulled out a WHSmith carrier bag from under the table and tipped it up so a pack of cards came tumbling out. "Fancy a game of Shed?"

"Why not." I took the cards and opened the plastic wrapping. After all, it looked like we were going to be stuck there a while.

If the train to Crewe had been quiet, the train from Crewe to Carlisle was the complete opposite – presumably because the one before it had been cancelled and everyone had crowded on to this one. Meg and I fought our way through with our bags – her first, because she had fewer reservations about using her elbows – and managed to snag two seats at a table in the unreserved carriage. I heaved our bags into the overhead racks – conveniently forgetting to take out the book first – and settled myself into my seat.

"I'm starving," Meg said, as a couple took the seats across from us.

"I've got some crisps left somewhere."

I watched the man and woman opposite as they added their bags to ours. He had dark blond dreadlocks and she had a tattoo of a feather behind her right ear, and they were both laughing as they sat down. But what I noticed – what I couldn't keep my eyes off – was the way they were constantly touching each other. Like, nothing obvious most of the time. But when he reached up to put his bag on the rack, she had a hand at his hip, just resting there. And when she stood up to take off her coat, he was there helping her get her arms out in the cramped space. Even when they were both settled, he kept one arm round her shoulders and she kept one hand on his thigh.

I looked across at Megan, staring out of the window at the busy station platform, and the small space between us felt like a gulf. We weren't a couple. We'd barely even been friends, the last few years. And yet, here we were.

"Hi!" The woman with the feather tattoo stuck her free hand out across the table. I took it, after a moment's hesitation, and shook. "I'm Jade," she said, smiling widely. "And this is my man, Phoenix." The American twang seemed real, I thought.

"Phoenix," I repeated as I shook his hand, too, hoping I didn't sound too disbelieving. Who names a baby Phoenix?

"What brilliant names!" Meg said, shaking hands with considerably more enthusiasm than I had. Another reason why she didn't have trouble making friends. That natural energy vibrated out of her.

Jade grinned. "I have my parents to thank for mine. But Phoenix named himself." She said it like she was proud of his ability to pick the most obnoxious name in history.

"You know, rising from the ashes, born again, that kind of thing." Phoenix's accent wasn't American. If I had to guess, I'd go with Lancashire. "Plus the name my parents picked for me really sucked."

"Right," I said.

"Where are you guys going?" Megan asked.

Phoenix shrugged. "Not really sure. We've been touring around North Wales – you know, Anglesey and stuff. We were heading back to a mate's place for a few nights but we might just keep going, you know? Head north and see where the spirit takes us."

"I've always wanted to see Scotland," Jade added. "My family came from there, a long time ago. What about you guys?"

Suddenly the gap between me and Megan disappeared as she entangled her arms with mine and cosied up against my shoulder. "We're off to Gretna Green. We're getting married tomorrow!"

"Oh my gosh, that is so exciting!" Jade took a hand off Phoenix for a moment to clap with joy.

Phoenix reached across the table and slapped me on the shoulder. "Congrats, man. That's like, the best news." He made it sound like we'd been friends for years, as though people had been waiting for me and Megan to make it official. It felt weird – but also strangely sincere.

And I couldn't deny, it felt nice to have people on our side for once.

"So, how did you two meet?" Megan asked, as the train lurched out of the station.

Jade and Phoenix exchanged a glance then both started talking at once. From what I could gather, Jade had run away from college to travel the world and they'd met at a festival and been inseparable ever since.

"It was love at first sight," Jade said, staring adoringly

at Phoenix. I stole a quick glance across at Meg but she didn't look as incredulous as I'd expected her to. "My parents … they weren't pleased about me staying over here in Britain but they get that I have to find my own life and live it, you know?"

"That must be nice," Megan said, her mouth twisting up into a half smile.

"It is." Jade grinned. "Plus, I'm twenty-one now. There's not much they can do about it!"

Only three years older than me, four years older than Megan.

"Just as well," Phoenix said. I wondered what his real name was. "Because I couldn't live without you."

Jade made a soppy 'aw' noise and they kissed again. I looked away, not wanting to watch, but all I saw was Megan's hair against my shoulder and her body pressed against mine. Somehow that felt worse – even more intimate. And more of a lie than the fake name and over-the-top romance of our travelling companions.

"Does she remind you of Lizzie?" Megan murmured, next to my ear, and I made myself look at Jade again.

"Not really." Or at all. I frowned, studying Jade again. What did Megan see that I was missing? Lizzie would never have got a tattoo or run away and never gone home. Lizzie was always sensible.

Until that last night. *You don't understand,* she'd said. *I need to do this.*

Megan sighed, her breath warm against my neck. "I guess it's just that she seems so ... alive."

Maybe Megan missed her sister so much that she saw her everywhere, these days. What had she said, the night she proposed? *I look just like her.* She didn't, not really. But it seemed more and more like she was torn between wanting to be like Lizzie and pulling away to the other extreme.

I needed to talk to Megan about Lizzie. Needed to tell her the full story of the night she died. Even if I really didn't want to.

But the packed train to Carlisle wasn't the place.

"What about you guys?" Phoenix asked when he'd finished kissing his girlfriend. "How did you get together?"

Megan and I exchanged a look. "Do you want to...?" she asked.

I shook my head. "No, no. You go ahead." I half-dreaded to think what sort of story she'd come up with for us but it had to be better than the truth. Or anything I could invent, come to that.

"Well, we used to be next-door neighbours," Meg started, and I realized she was going for the truth. The truth with a twist, anyway. "So we grew up together – playing down the beach, that sort of thing. Then when we were eleven or so, Elliott's family moved away and we kind of drifted apart." She smiled up at me. "Until last year. We reconnected and... Well, the rest is history."

"Aw, that's so sweet! You guys were childhood sweethearts and now you're getting married!"

Jade and Phoenix didn't seem to have clocked that we were kind of young to be getting married, so I didn't draw attention to it. I guess if you believe in love at first sight, anything seems possible.

Beside me, Meg pulled out her camera. "Do you mind?" she asked. "Only, I'm a photographer and I'm always looking to build up my portfolio. And you two are just so gorgeous together..."

"Go ahead!" Jade pulled a pose, Phoenix laughed and the camera started to click as Megan took shot after shot, each more ridiculous.

I wondered if I could retrieve *Eloping with the Earl* from the bag without Megan noticing. But instead I settled back to watch Megan at work, pulling a face when she turned the camera on me.

"Gosh, look!" Jade pointed out of the window and we all turned.

The rumblings of conversation that had been building

in the carriage spilled over as we all realized what was happening. It was snowing.

Huge white flakes fell from the sky, fat and fateful. I stared out as the landscape around us turned white. It must have been snowing for a while in this area because it got deeper and deeper the further north we got.

"It's beautiful," Jade murmured.

Megan caught my eye. "What do you think?"

"Check the app," I suggested. "See if they've updated it yet."

"What are you guys talking about?" Jade asked.

"The trains," Phoenix explained.

"Nothing yet," Meg said, staring at her phone.

All around us, people were discussing what had happened last time it snowed so heavily on this line and who'd been stuck where. For the first time, fear seeped into my bones. If we were going to get stranded in the middle of nowhere in the snow...

Megan's hand slipped into mine and I squeezed her fingers for reassurance.

"It'll be OK," she whispered, just as the train announcement system crackled into life.

Due to the inclement weather, this train will be terminating at our next stop: Oxenholme, the Lake District. Next and final stop, Oxenholme.

Megan

Back at home, sitting at the counter in Oracle and coming up with plans with Becca, I thought we'd covered all the bases. I honestly believed we'd come up with a plan that couldn't fail. Except I hadn't considered shoddy mechanics or the British weather.

"We're definitely going to miss our connection now," I said, looking up at Elliott. He looked even more deflated than I felt.

"We're going to be stranded in a train station in the middle of nowhere overnight," he said. "I think the missed train is the least of our worries."

Which was true. The plan said go to Gretna. The twin room in the cheap hotel we had booked for the night and paid for in advance was in Gretna.

And we were in the Lake District. Snowed in.

"Hey, do you guys have somewhere to go tonight?" Jade asked, frowning with concern across the table.

I exchanged another glance with Elliott. He gave me a tiny shake of the head, an indication that he'd rather go it alone, I guessed. But what other options did we have?

"Not yet," I said, as brightly as I could. "But I'm sure we'll come up with something."

"You can come with us, if you like," Phoenix offered, shrugging on his coat.

"Where?" Elliott asked with a frown. I wondered if he was still thinking about what Phoenix's real name had been. I knew it was bugging him. Me, I just admired his ability to start over.

"This area's kind of my patch. I know a place," Phoenix said vaguely. "We can get a bed for the night for free at least. Then maybe the trains will be running in the morning. Or we could get a lift from a mate, perhaps. I'll make some calls."

"That's … really kind of you." It was dubious-sounding, but kind.

"Well, we can't have you guys missing your own wedding, can we?" Jade laughed. "Besides, you'll need witnesses, right?"

"I think the venue——" Elliott began, but Jade ignored him.

"Maybe even a best man and a maid of honour…"

She nudged Phoenix in the ribs.

"Happy to help," Phoenix said with a grin. "I've never been a best man."

It wasn't in the plan but it was the best offer we had. "If you can get us to our wedding on time, you'll be our best man and woman ever," I told them.

By the time we'd tramped a mile or two in the cold and the dark and the snow, I was feeling rather less charitable towards our new friends.

"Do you even have any idea where they're taking us?" Elliott muttered, as he caught my elbow to stop me stumbling into another snow-filled pothole.

"Somewhere warm. With beds. And maybe even food." I clung on to his arm to keep my balance on the slippery road. "I figure that's better than anything else that was on offer."

"If we make it there alive."

"Don't say it." I knew exactly where he was going with this.

"They could be murderers!" I don't know how it was possible to shout while whispering but Elliott managed it. "We only met them a handful of hours ago. We know nothing about them."

"Elliott, trust me. Your life is not interesting enough for you to get kidnapped by serial killers."

"Ha!" Elliott almost lost his footing as he laughed. "Up until the point where I decided to elope with you, I'd probably have agreed."

"So I'm the most interesting thing in your life?"

"By far."

Eventually we reached a large white sign, welcoming us to Sunny Waters caravan park.

"Here?" Elliott asked. "You guys own a caravan?"

Jade and Phoenix exchanged a look. "Not exactly," Jade admitted. She looked a little guilty.

"But we do know how to borrow one for the night," Phoenix said. "Trust us. The park is closed, there's no one here and all these potential homes are just going to waste. It's a public service, really."

Even I wasn't convinced of the logic of that one, so I knew Elliott definitely wouldn't be. Still, it was bloody freezing and we *did* need somewhere to sleep.

"Let's get going, then," I said, without looking at Elliott. "Show us to our room!"

Phoenix clapped his hands together with a muffled, gloved sound. "Right! Let's go!"

Elliott grabbed my arm and held me back. "Are you sure about this?"

"Not at all," I said, shivering. "But we're here now. What else are we going to do? We can't walk all the way back to the station in this snow."

"I suppose not." He didn't look happy about it but he didn't stop me hurrying after them, either.

The caravan Jade and Phoenix picked was towards the middle of the park, hidden behind a clump of trees, which suggested to me they weren't quite as confident about the place being abandoned as they'd suggested. But since it was already nearly midnight and we needed to be gone first thing to get to Gretna in time, I figured we had a good chance of getting away with it.

Phoenix did something to the lock on the door that made Elliott wince. Despite everything, I'd realized over the last month that this grown-up Elliott hadn't changed that much from the boy I'd known. He still wanted to do the right thing. He was determined not to do anything to make him like his dad.

After a few seconds, the door swung open and we all bundled through. Inside the caravan was about as cold as it was outside, just without the wind and snow.

"Electrics and gas won't be on," Phoenix said. "But there's usually a few torches and plenty of blankets."

Jade rummaged around in a drawer in the tiny

kitchen and pulled out two torches. "Here." She tossed one to Elliott, who caught it one-handed.

"And even better…" Phoenix held up a bottle of red wine from the wine rack and a packet of biscuits from the bread bin. "Sustenance!"

Elliott's mouth was fixed into a firm, straight line but he didn't say anything as Jade and Phoenix opened the wine and the biscuits. I guessed that, whatever his moral objections, he was as hungry as I was. That sandwich in Crewe seemed a long time ago already.

"Come on, Meg," Jade said, after a swig of wine. "Let's find some blankets."

The caravan had three bedrooms and cupboards filled with extra sleeping bags and towels, so in the end we managed to gather up two double duvets, four singles and three sleeping bags to keep us warm.

"You guys *must* take the double room," Jade said, as we all huddled under the pile of blankets in the lounge, taking turns to drink from the bottle and handing around the biscuits. Phoenix was in the corner, the edge of a sleeping bag pulled over his lap, on the phone to a mate who might have a car, apparently. "I mean, it's the night before your wedding."

Elliott shook his head. "You found the caravan. We'll be fine in one of the twin rooms. Won't we, Meg?"

"Absolutely," I agreed. Although I couldn't help but think it might be warmer in the double with Elliott to cuddle up to.

Not that I was imagining cuddling up to Elliott. Much.

OK, just a bit. Maybe it was watching Phoenix and Jade together – the way they were always touching, like they couldn't bear to be more than a few centimetres apart. I'd never had that with anyone.

I wondered if I even wanted it. I quite liked being able to do my own thing whenever I felt like it.

But to have someone, like they had each other … that would be nice.

"No arguments," Jade said firmly. "You guys take the double."

"Great. We'll see you in the morning. Thanks, sis!" Phoenix stabbed the end call button with his finger and grinned at us as Jade handed him the wine. "That's our lift sorted. Hannah will be here at nine."

"Hannah?" Elliott asked.

"My sister," Phoenix explained. "She owes me a favour. She's a vet up by the border so she's always driving around this area."

"Nine?" I was more concerned about the time than the relationship. "Will that get us to Gretna in time?"

"The way Hannah drives? No problem!"

"Don't worry, guys," Jade added. "You guys are just *meant* to get married tomorrow. I can feel it. You'll get there in time. It's, like, fate."

Fate. I was pretty sure no mystical power, even one as powerful as fate, would have been able to predict me and Elliott getting married. But if fate wanted to be on our side for now, I had no objections.

Phoenix, Jade, fate and maybe Becca. That was quite a team of cheerleaders Elliott and I had.

The wine didn't last long between four of us and it was already late, so as Jade drained the last mouthful I said, "Maybe we should get to bed. I mean, if Hannah's picking us up at nine…"

"Of course!" Jade jumped to her feet, sending biscuit crumbs and blankets flying. "You want to be well rested for your big day!"

"And *you* probably want to get some practice in for the big night," Phoenix said, winking at Elliott.

Elliott ignored him.

"Come on," Jade said. "Let's get you almost-weds all tucked in for the night."

The double bedroom of the caravan was barely bigger than the bed itself, which was smaller than any double bed I'd seen before. Elliott and I didn't bother undressing – it was too cold for that – but we dug out our toothbrushes and made use of the tiny en-suite bathroom one at a time. There was no way we'd both fit in there at once and it felt weird enough preparing for bed with Elliott without squeezing past him to get to the sink. Actually going to bed with him felt even weirder – even if there were still four layers of clothes, a sleeping bag and two duvets between us.

Soon, I realized, this would be my new reality. Well, not the sharing a bed thing, but sharing space. Seeing Elliott at all those times of day I'd only ever really seen my family before.

As we huddled down under the covers, the only light in the room coming from the moon through a gap between the curtains, I heard Jade and Phoenix giggling in the next room. I wondered if they were holding hands across the gap between their twin beds. Probably, I decided. Even if they had to keep their gloves on to do it.

"Do you think we'll make it to Gretna in time?" I whispered, wriggling a little closer to Elliott.

"I hope so," he murmured back. "We've come a long way for nothing, otherwise."

"For nothing? Do you really think so?"

"Maybe not nothing," Elliott admitted. "I mean,

there was wine and biscuits. And a lot more hiking than I expected on an imaginary hiking trip."

"That's not what I meant." I poked him in the ribs and he grabbed my hand under the duvet to stop me.

"I know," Elliott said softly, squeezing my hand tight before letting go. "I couldn't go back now, even if I wanted to. To St Evaline, I mean. Whatever happens … that's not the place for me any more."

We'd both changed since the night I proposed to him. And even if we never made it to Gretna … I wouldn't want to give up those changes.

Or Elliott.

I thought hard, trying to figure out what Elliott meant to me now. Was he my best friend again? Or a hot guy I sometimes imagined kissing? Or … or was there really something else between us?

"Elliott?" I breathed his name, just wanting to know he was still awake.

It took a few seconds but then he shifted on to his side, mirroring me, his eyes shining in the almost blackness.

"Hey," he said. He was so close I could feel his warm breath on my skin.

"Hey," I echoed. Because, really, what was a girl supposed to say at a moment like this?

For a long time we just stared at each other, like we were memorizing the lines and shadows of each other's faces in the darkness. Drinking each other in, saving the moment for the future – for the morning, when all would be bright and snowy white, and moments like this simply couldn't happen.

And I knew I didn't have to memorize anything. There wasn't a chance of me forgetting a second of this night.

"Megan…" he started, then stopped.

"What is it?" I whispered.

"There's something I've been meaning to talk to you about," he said eventually. "Like, ever since you proposed. But I couldn't figure out how. And now it's the night before our wedding and … I'm out of time."

A shiver that had nothing to do with the cold ran through me and I tried to sit up but he tugged me back down, wrapping an arm round me until I was closer to him than I'd been since we started this whole adventure.

"Don't … don't go anywhere," he said, and I was close enough to see the worry in his eyes in the pale moonlight. "Please."

"OK."

"It's about Lizzie."

A million possibilities flew through my head. But for once, I waited and let him speak.

"You asked me about the night she died," he said, and I could tell from his voice that this was going to be awful. "And I know you've already heard all the facts in court. But you wanted to know how she was feeling. What she was thinking, that night, to get on that boat with Evan..."

I swallowed and it hurt my throat. "You told me she was celebrating finishing her exams."

His eyes fluttered closed, like he couldn't look at me as he said it. "I lied."

I didn't want to hear this, whatever it was. But something inside me *needed* to know. "What happened?"

Elliott shifted slightly, pulling me closer into his arms, my head against his chest, meaning I couldn't see his face as he spoke.

"When I got down to the cove that night, I could tell something was different." Already, it sounded unlike the story he'd told in court – that one had been more like a list of bullet points, the facts and nothing but the facts. This version was the night as Elliott had experienced it. "Lizzie was ... she was manic, bouncing all over the place, talking to everyone. For a moment, I almost thought she was—" He broke off.

"Drunk?" I guessed.

"You," he said softly.

"Oh."

"I went to talk to her and it didn't take long to realize that she wasn't herself. Someone handed her a drink and she took it, and downed it without even looking what it was. I tried to stick with her, to look after her, but she didn't want me there. She kept saying she was older than me. That she didn't need protecting. That she was sick of doing what everyone expected of her."

That much, I could understand. But Lizzie? She'd always seemed more than happy to follow the accepted path.

I stayed quiet and Elliott carried on.

"I got her alone eventually and asked her what was going on. I said, why didn't I call you, and you could come down and hang out with us, too. And she ... she laughed. But it wasn't like her normal laugh. It sounded ... bitter, I guess."

"We'd had an argument that night," I said, the memories still fresh. "Before I went out. I'd said some stuff." Untrue, unkind things. Words I'd take back in an instant, if I could.

I hadn't known that would be the last time I'd ever see her alive.

"I know," Elliott said, and I froze in his arms. "She told me."

The thought of Elliott knowing all the terrible things I'd said – and done – that night filled me with horror. Swallowing the lump in my throat I asked, "What? What did she say?"

"She told me... She was drunk by this point, remember. I don't think she'd have said anything, otherwise. And as far as I know she didn't tell anyone else."

"Just say it," I whispered.

"She said that you'd gone out to sleep with Dylan that night. That it was..."

"My first time," I finished for him as he trailed off awkwardly. "Yeah. I did."

"It's none of my business, anyway." Elliott's arms felt stiff around me.

"What else did she say?" I asked, feeling uncomfortable with the conversation.

Elliott sighed. "She said ... she said that you were right. That she didn't know how to live. You were out there living your life while she was stuck inside even though the exams were over."

"She already had the reading list for the course she hoped to take at Oxford," I said, remembering the stack of books on her desk. "She said it was important to get ahead."

"I lost track of her for a while after that and the next time I saw her she was with Evan Roberts and his mates." Elliott paused. We both knew what happened next. "They were daring her to do stuff – kiss someone, down another shot, stuff like that. Then Evan announced he wanted to take a boat trip. Lizzie said she wasn't sure and they laughed at her. Dared her to."

"And she said yes." I could see it happening in my mind, like an awful movie I couldn't switch off.

"I tried to stop them taking the boat out," Elliott went on. "I told them it was too rough, too dangerous. They'd been drinking, they didn't know what they were doing … but they wouldn't listen to me. I called the coastguard, the police, anyone who'd listen but…"

"They were too late." The boat had smashed against the rolling waves and Lizzie had fallen overboard, whacking her head so she was unconscious as she sank to the bottom of the sea. It had been hours before they found her body, tangled in seaweed. "You were part of the search party, weren't you?" I said, lifting my head so I could see him. His face was tight with pain.

"Yeah. I was there when they brought her in."

"I'm sorry," I said. "That must have been horrible. But ... I'm glad you were there. I know ... I know you think it didn't make a difference. But it does to me. You were there for her and she knew that. That matters."

"Maybe. But Meg ... I spoke to her, one last time, before she got on the boat." Elliott's voice sounded hoarse, like the words were painful to speak. "I begged her not to go with them. But she said..."

"What? What did she say?" My sister's almost-last words.

He paused for too long before answering.

"Tell me. Please." I knew that they would hurt but I had to hear them all the same.

"She said she was sick of you having all the fun. She said she needed to prove that she could have fun, too. That she wasn't just perfect Lizzie. That she could be impulsive, like you. That she was going to live her life the way you did."

Like you. The words hit me in the heart and I let out a sob.

"Oh God." It was my fault. Lizzie had, for one dreadful moment, wanted to be like me. And it had killed her.

Sorrow swamped me and I let the tears fall.

All the tears I'd held back for the last year, since I had managed to stop crying every morning when I remembered she was gone.

"She was better than me," I whispered between sobs. "She was so much nicer. Cleverer. Everything. And I can't ever live up to that. I just want her to be here."

"You don't have to be Lizzie. You have to be yourself," Elliott said fiercely. "That's more than enough, Meg."

"Is it?" Then why was it such a battle? Why did I have to fight every step of the way?

"I should have told you before," Elliott said, wrapping his arms more tightly round me, holding me close against his chest. "I should have found you and told you. But you were so angry with me…"

"I shouldn't have been. It was my fault. Not yours."

"No," he said sharply. "It was Evan Roberts's fault – he took out that boat, drunk. He caused Lizzie's accident."

"Yeah, maybe."

"I should have told you," Elliott said again.

I shook my head. "No. No, I needed to hear this now. Here. This is right."

"Just promise me you won't blame yourself," he said,

and I nodded, not really sure if I was telling the truth.

Elliott kissed the top of my head and let me cry for a while, just holding me.

"What about you?" I asked eventually, when the tears had passed. "Who are you trying to be?"

Elliott didn't answer for a moment but his arms loosened a little. "I guess … I've always tried to *not* be my father. That was all. Not who everyone expected me to be."

"And now?"

"Now I want to start fresh. Somewhere that's not St Evaline." He sounded almost optimistic about it.

"You're going to rise from the ashes, like a phoenix?" I joked feebly. "You'll need a new name for that…"

"How about … husband?" he asked. "Still want to marry me tomorrow?"

He stared into my eyes as he spoke and I stared back, feeling a connection that went so much deeper than I'd imagined possible the night I'd proposed.

"Yes," I said and, for a second, I thought he might kiss me. I could feel the anticipation of it running through my exhausted body.

But he didn't.

Instead he looked away. "We should get some sleep."

"We should." But I didn't want to. I wanted to lie

like this, staring at Elliott. I wanted to move closer.
I wanted…

Oh God.

I wanted to kiss him. I wanted to do more than kiss
him. And I wanted everything.

Everything.

The realization ran through me like an echo
repeated over and over and over until you can't hear
anything else.

"Good night, Megan." Elliott moved, reaching out
to close the gap in the curtains, and the room plunged
into the sort of total, utter darkness you can only get in
a caravan in the middle of nowhere.

But it felt like my new knowledge was lighting up
the room.

"Good night," I whispered, and wondered how I was
ever going to sleep.

Sean

Decline

Accept

Sean: Hey, Becca? OK, I've slept on it, like you asked. And if you really won't let me tell Mum, then I need to go after them. I have to stop Elliott making a ginormous mistake.

Becca: Sean, you can't. You probably wouldn't even get there in time. The chance of your car even making it that far—

Sean: Hey, it's fixed. Iain says it's fine. And I've got to do something.

Becca: Why? Isn't it their mistake to make?

Sean: Because he's my brother. Because this is his future. Because I want him to be happy and this sure as hell isn't going to make him happy.

Becca: You don't know that.

Sean: OK, be honest. Do you really think those two are going to get married and live happily ever after?

[SILENCE]

Sean: That's what I thought. I'm going to tell Mum.

Becca: No. No, Sean, you can't. Just … wait. I'm coming over, right now.

Elliott

The light through the flimsy caravan curtains was too bright for winter. Beside me Megan stirred and I froze, waiting to see if she was properly awake. She burrowed deeper into the pillow and pulled a blanket over her head. I relaxed.

I had spent the night with Megan Hughes. And although it wasn't exactly the hot night anyone would imagine if I told them this story, for a second there, I'd thought she wanted to kiss me.

That hadn't happened, of course. It couldn't.

I checked my watch – it was already gone half eight. If Phoenix's sister Hannah was coming at nine, we really needed to get moving.

"Up and at 'em, lovebirds!" Jade's voice rang out, and Megan's head emerged from under the blanket.

"It's time to go?" she asked, her voice soft from sleep and her eyes barely open.

"Yeah." My own voice came out scratchy.

Megan sat up, wiping at her eyes, and the nearness of her made me lose my breath.

Lurching out of bed, I muttered something about the bathroom and headed into the tiny en-suite to get away from all the stuff I knew I shouldn't be feeling.

I stared at myself in the streaky mirror, trying to find my sensible self again. The realistic Elliott who knew UCL was a dream he couldn't have. The cynical Elliott who realized that Megan was only using him to get what she wanted. The pessimistic Elliott who'd expected the whole plan to fall apart from the start.

Except now it was my wedding day. And I really, really wanted to kiss my fiancée.

But I couldn't. Even if Meg went for it … it would be the worst idea ever. We'd drive each other crazy in a week – especially if we were living together in London. And then she'd kick me out, marriage certificate or not. The only way I could do London and UCL was if I could live with Megan and save on rent. And the only way I could live with Megan was not to kiss her and ruin everything we'd planned.

I shook my head. I was overthinking this. It was just being near each other all the time and the excitement of the plan.

I tried to make myself believe that.

When I opened the door, Megan had already folded up our blankets and Phoenix was stashing them back where they belonged. Jade brushed up the remaining biscuit crumbs and popped the empty packet and the bottle in a carrier bag to take with us.

Then Megan's phone rang.

"Becca? What's up? Sorry, my battery's nearly dead and there's no electric here so I turned it off... Wait. What? How?!" Across the tiny caravan lounge, Megan tensed up so hard I thought she might shatter.

"What's happened?" I asked in an urgent whisper.

"Wait, so what's happening now? Becca? Bec?!" Meg lowered the phone. "Battery's gone."

"What's going on?" I asked again, just as Jade said from the kitchen, "Is everything OK, guys?"

"Your mum knows." Meg met my gaze as she spoke, her eyes wide with worry.

"What? How?"

"Sean pestered Becca until she told him the truth." Meg sighed. "Apparently they can't argue quietly because your mum overheard them. Becca's been trying to call me for the last two hours. And that's not the worst of it."

"God, what else?"

"Your mum told my parents. They're on their way."

Meg bit her bottom lip, trying to stop herself crying. "El, they're going to stop us. They're going to ruin all our plans and dictate every tiny thing I do for the rest of my life until I turn into Lizzie. I can't! I'm not her! This was my one chance and we've blown it. I just..." Her eyes filled with tears and I reached across to grab hold of her shoulders.

"Breathe, Meg." The more panicked she got, the calmer I felt. So, everyone knew. Who cared? We were hundreds of miles away. We were still ahead of them. "It's going to take them, what? Five, six hours to get to Gretna from Cardiff? More if the roads are really bad. Even if they left two hours ago, we're only an hour or two away. We're going to beat them."

"But the wedding isn't until this afternoon," Meg said nervously. "What if they get there before then?"

"They won't," I said with confidence. "We're nearly there. We've got this."

I stared into her eyes, my hands still tight on her shoulders, and watched her panic fade. We were in this together.

And for a moment, it felt just like it had the night before. The urge to lean in, to kiss her, was almost overwhelming. The world had shrunk to just the two of us and the potential that stretched between us, tight and taut and growing...

I stepped away.

"Come on," I said. "It's nearly time."

On our way out, when I was sure no one was watching, I slipped my last couple of fivers under the edge of the bread bin, for whoever owned the caravan.

Megan

We hung around at the edge of the caravan park, waiting for Hannah to arrive. Jade tossed snowballs at Phoenix, trying to get Elliott to join in, but he wouldn't. I tramped out into the road to watch for cars forcing their way through the snow.

There weren't many. But I couldn't shake the thought that the next one might be my parents, whatever Elliott said about bad roads and driving times – or the fact that they couldn't possibly know we were in a caravan park in the middle of nowhere.

It would be just like my parents to flout the laws of space and time just to stop me doing what I wanted.

Beyond the small side road where the caravan site was located, though, the major roads seemed to have been cleared. The snow had stopped in the night and, according to Jade's phone, we weren't due any more. If Hannah arrived on time, we might still manage this.

She didn't. She arrived at quarter to ten, by which time we were all freezing and enjoying the snow even less.

"Sorry!" She tossed her dark plaited hair over her shoulder as she smiled at us through the window of her beaten-up old Jeep. "Got held up rescuing a sheep from a fence. But I'm here now! Where we off to?"

"Gretna!" Jade jumped into the back of the Jeep, while Phoenix took the passenger seat next to Hannah. Elliott and I followed Jade, perching on the precarious bench seats in the back. Elliott was looking very dubious about our mode of transport. "We've got a couple of lovebirds we need to get married today."

"Sounds beautiful!" The Jeep crunched and ground its way through a three-point turn in the snow and back out on to the main road.

Even on the cleared roads, progress was slower than I'd like. Elliott kept checking his watch every few seconds, as if that could make us go faster.

I pulled out my camera to pass the time, scrolling through the photos I'd taken since our road trip began. Scenery shots to start with – the Brecons through the car window, Elliott's back as he trudged down the hill to the village in the rain. The pub sign, the village shop with the hills in the background. Then people.

There were photos of Jeffrey and Bill and the landlady in The Red Dragon. Jeffrey standing proudly beside his tractor. Elliott waiting at the train station, holding *Eloping with the Earl*. The crowds waiting for the delayed and cancelled trains at Crewe. Jade and Phoenix, kissing on the train, drinking wine in the caravan last night. The peaceful blanket of snow outside while we waited for Hannah that morning, Jade and Phoenix throwing snowballs in the middle of it.

"You make them look alive," Jade said softly and I realized she'd been watching over my shoulder. "The people in your photos. They all look like they might move or talk or laugh at any second."

"Thanks," I whispered, staring at the last photo I'd taken – of Elliott, rolling his eyes as I turned the camera on him.

When I thought back to the photos of seashells and driftwood I'd tried to convince the local gallery to sell, I was almost embarrassed. How had I never seen what *mattered* in my photos before? I'd been basing my photos on the glossy books I'd studied or the travel blogs I'd followed – never realizing that the photos I connected with were the ones with people in them.

It had taken escaping from St Evaline to show me what I really wanted to capture.

I switched off my camera. It felt like I had to start learning all over again – to rethink everything I knew. Like yesterday, when I'd suddenly had to see Lizzie's last night through new eyes – Elliott's eyes.

Perhaps the world we thought we knew was always changing, the truth always shifting. And all we could do was capture the moments.

"You'll have to email me that one of me and Phoenix. Once you get back home, I mean," Jade said, and I smiled.

"Sure."

Finally we passed a sign welcoming us to Scotland and we all started to relax. We were almost there – this was the last leg.

"OK, I need fuel." Hannah swung off the main road into a service station, provoking a series of beeps from the cars behind us. She waved away my offer of money, saying, "You're practically on my way. And I owe Henry – sorry, Phoenix – anyway. He's been running interference with our parents for me." She sighed. "They are *not* happy about my new girlfriend."

Henry. So that was his real name. I glanced over at Phoenix, taking in the dreads and the rough woven top he was wearing. No wonder he changed it. Phoenix was *not* a Henry. Hannah seemed like the perfect daughter by comparison – respectable job, normal hair. But I guess parents could always find something to complain about.

I watched Elliott as the car pulled to a halt. He'd been quiet the whole journey so far. Jade had given us a couple of worried looks but otherwise left us to ourselves, which I appreciated.

I had a lot to think about.

Despite everything, I *had* slept last night. And dreamed. And imagined.

And while I might have been able to pass last night's feelings off as just being in the moment … I couldn't do that about this morning. The way he'd looked at me. The intensity when he'd stared into my eyes. His hands on my shoulders, calming me down…

He'd wanted to kiss me, too. I was sure of it.

So why hadn't he?

I needed a moment alone with him to find out what this was.

"Last chance for the loo before Gretna!" Hannah sang, and we all piled out of the Jeep to head for the services.

It didn't take too much effort to catch Elliott alone, grabbing his arm while the others joined the queue for the coffee shop.

"You don't want a coffee?" he asked, barely looking at me. "Because I really need caffeine and it's bloody freezing out here."

"Actually I wanted to talk." That made him glance up.

"Now? About what?"

I looked into his eyes and realized: I didn't want to talk at all.

Whatever was going on between us, dancing around it wasn't going to help. We could talk all day long and not say anything that mattered. Plus, we were running out of time. I needed to know what this was before I said 'I do'.

Stretching up on my tiptoes, I rested one hand against his chest and pressed my lips to his. And then I did it again, gasping as he kissed me back, and my whole body trembled.

But then Elliott pulled away, frown lines etched into his forehead.

"What was that?" he asked, his voice hard.

My heart seemed to shrink inside my ribcage. Had I read this wrong? I'd been so sure last night... Had I misread comfort for something else? And now Elliott was looking like he was about to run. I couldn't risk that.

I didn't have time to feel embarrassed or disappointed or upset.

I had to put things back the way they were before. To convince Elliott that nothing had changed, that we should still get married, stick to the plan.

"An experiment," I said, aiming for breezy indifference. "Nothing to worry about."

I tried to turn away but he grabbed my arm, holding me close enough that he could look into my eyes. I kept my smile bright even though my cheeks were aching.

"No, Meg," he said softly. "Just ... no."

Then he let me go and walked through the doors to the service station as if nothing had happened at all.

Maybe it hadn't, for him.

But for me ... that kiss had told me everything I needed to know about how I felt about Elliott.

That kiss changed everything.

Elliott

She kissed me.

She only went and bloody kissed me.

Why? An experiment? Because she felt whatever it was between us last night, too?

It didn't matter, I decided, as I climbed into the back of Hannah's Jeep. Whatever her reasons, it was a bad idea.

Except ... before the kiss I hadn't known what it would feel like. How perfectly her lips fitted against mine. How the whole world slowed down when she touched me.

No. I wasn't going there. Not when we were so close to getting what we wanted.

Whether Megan realized it or not, our future in London depended on us being friends. Not girlfriend and boyfriend. Not lovers.

We had to be able to live together, without drama,

without stress. I couldn't risk the security that our marriage and our flat would give me for anything else.

Being with Megan … that was one dream that definitely couldn't come true.

Sean

 Decline   Accept

Becca: Hey. Where are you?

Sean: Halfway to Scotland, I reckon. What time did you say the wedding was booked for?

Becca: Three o'clock.

Sean: Still a chance I might make it, then.

Becca: Yeah.

Sean: I mean, it would be nice to get there before my brother ruins his life.

Becca: Sean...

Sean: What? You're sorry for not telling me the truth sooner? For helping my brother ruin his life? What?

Becca: I'm sorry you're taking this out on me, mostly.

Sean: Who else would I take it out on? Honestly, Bec, I thought we had something. I thought we could trust each other. That we could talk...

Becca: Seriously? When did we ever talk about anything that mattered to me? We flirted, we kissed, we texted... When did we talk, Sean?

Sean: We talked!

Becca: Sure, about abstract stuff! About your dad, about my parents, about our plans. But about whether we were really dating? Um, no. About how we felt about each other? Definitely not. About why you said more to me by text than in person? Why you practically ignored me whenever your friends were around? No and no. So why the hell would I tell you something I promised my friends I'd keep a secret? At least I know how they feel about me.

Sean: And how is that? That you're a useful person to have about when you need someone to lie for you?

Becca: That's not true.

Sean: Are you sure? Seems like that to me.

Becca: Goodbye, Sean.

Sean: Yeah. I need to get back on the road anyway.

[PAUSE]

Becca: Drive safe.

Sean: I'm just driving to get there in time.

Megan

After everything – all the delays, the weather, the breakdowns – we made it to Gretna with time to kill before our slot.

Phoenix hugged Hannah and we all said our grateful thank yous, which she waved off as nothing. Then the Jeep roared off again into the snow, leaving us standing on the edge of Gretna Green, staring at an apparently famous Blacksmith's shop – complete with shopping centre, café, playground and something called a 'courtship maze'.

"This is it?" Elliott asked.

I checked the paperwork one last time. "This is it."

We registered our arrival and Jade insisted we have a poke around, getting, as she said, 'a feel for the place'.

"It's perfect!" Jade clapped her hands together as we met up in the Gretna Green shop. "If Nix and I ever get married, I want it to be right here. And we're just in time to get you all prettied up, ready to be a bride!"

I gave her a weak smile. She was so excited to be part of our big day. At this point, how did I even tell her it was all a show? A scheme. Especially since I was starting to wish that it wasn't.

Phoenix handed me my rucksack from where I'd dumped it on the floor. "I guess this probably has all the essentials in it? Shoes, dress, rings, that sort of thing."

"Yeah," I said, taking it from him. With all the snow outside, I'd decided it was best to get ready at the venue. I dug into the front pocket. "I suppose I'd better give you the rings," I said, feeling around for the small ring box I'd watched Becca put in there the previous day. We'd picked up the cheapest plain bands that Argos had to offer, in approximately the right sizes, in the Boxing Day sale.

But there was no ring box in the bag.

Panicked, I rifled through the main part of the bag, pulling everything out on to the shop floor, but still no sign. "They're not here!"

"Don't worry about it," Elliott said, way more calm than I'd expected. Almost detached.

"Don't worry? We need rings, Elliott. They must have got lost when I was getting things out somewhere. Maybe on the train…"

"Megan. It doesn't matter." He started methodically putting things back into the bag for me.

"Yes, it does!" He jerked away from me as I tried to grab his hands. I stared up at him, desperately trying to understand the new dynamic between us – and failing.

Elliott stuck a hand in his pocket and pulled out a small paper bag folded up into an even smaller square. Tossing it to me he said, "No, it doesn't. See? Sorted."

My hands shook as I unfolded the paper, pulling out a thin, silver band studded with tiny sparkling stones. "It's beautiful." I slid it on to my ring finger. "A perfect fit."

It looked like it belonged there. Like I was meant to wear it forever. But when I glanced up, Elliott wasn't even looking at me. He'd chosen me this perfect ring and now he couldn't even meet my eyes.

"You can't wear it yet!" Jade grabbed my hand and tugged the ring from my finger, handing it to Phoenix. "The best man has to look after it until the ceremony."

"What about you?" I asked Elliott, wishing the distance between us didn't feel so much bigger than it had that morning. "You don't have a ring."

He shrugged. "They're not compulsory for guys, anyway."

But he'd gone out and chosen one for me. I doubted it was expensive or that the sparkles were real diamonds but that didn't matter. Even though it was all a lie, Elliott had gone and bought me a ring.

Suddenly, I got the feeling I was missing something. Something big.

"You should go and get ready," Elliott said, turning away, and I nodded numbly.

"Let me know if Becca calls."

I followed Jade past the shops and towards the toilets, still thinking.

What if Elliott hadn't been as unmoved by that kiss as I'd thought?

Elliott

I left Phoenix in deep discussion with one of the cashiers in the food hall about the true meaning of marriage and headed back outside to get some air. Some cold, numbing air.

We were getting married. I was almost sure that even if Meg's parents were on their way, they wouldn't be able to get here on time. And if they did, could they really stop us? If this was what we wanted, it was our decision, whatever Meg thought. They couldn't make her do anything.

It was almost funny. She was so determined to live her own life but when it came down to it, she was scared she'd give in to her parents and she felt she had to elope to avoid it. Was that better or worse than me? Refusing to even *let* myself dream about my future.

"Mate," Phoenix called from the door. "You wanna see this. Trust me."

I took a last gulp of cold air and headed back with him.

Meg stood by the doors, wearing a dress covered in lace that looked like snowflakes. It left her arms bare and ended just below her knees, above her silver high heels. She'd pinned her blond curls back with sparkly clips and her lips looked more kissable than ever.

She looked beautiful. Perfect.

"You look—" I started, but before I could find the words, the shouting started behind Meg.

"What do you mean, there's no photographer?" a distraught woman in a wedding dress cried.

"I'm very sorry, miss, but you didn't book the package with a photographer. If there was one available, I'm sure you could upgrade, but I'm afraid all our photographers are currently engaged at other venues."

"But it's my wedding!" the bride sobbed and threw herself on to her groom's shoulder.

"Is there really nothing you can do?" the groom asked. "Only, I'd hate not to have any mementos of our big day..."

"Well, if you've got a camera phone," the man from the venue started, and the bride sobbed louder.

Then Jade crossed the room and put one arm round the bride. "Don't worry," she was saying. "The universe is on your side."

The bride blinked up at her in confusion. "The universe?"

Jade nodded, smiling widely. "It just so happens that our friend here is a photographer. I'm sure that she'll help you out, won't you, Meg?"

Megan glanced at me uncertainly, but she stepped towards them anyway. "Um, sure. If you want—"

"Yes! Please!" the groom said quickly.

"I'd love to," Meg said, more firmly this time.

It was weird sitting at the back of the ceremony room, watching Meg work and knowing that in just a short while it would be us up there. We didn't have a photographer either, of course, but that didn't matter. Our wedding didn't need mementos. All it needed was to be legally binding.

The bride's tears were dry now as she beamed for the camera. Meg darted around capturing angles I'd never have thought of.

She was clearly in her element.

The ceremony was over much faster than I'd expected. Meg took a few more shots of the happy couple standing over the famous Blacksmith's anvil, then headed out to take some photos of them in the snow.

"Ten minutes?" the registrar said to me, with what I imagined was supposed to be an encouraging smile.

"Great." If this had been a normal wedding, our guests would be arriving now, filing in to take their seats.

As it was, the room was empty.

I sat alone at the back of the ceremony room, my head tipped back against the cool wall, my eyes closed, and waited. Weeks of planning and we were here at last.

We were getting married.

Finally the door opened and there was Megan.

"Are you sure you want to do this?" she asked. "Because you keep giving me all these chances to back out and I realized, I never gave you that chance. Mostly because I was scared you might take it. But we're here now and this is it. So this is me giving you that chance." The words tumbled out of her. Then she bit her lip, standing watching me from the doorway.

"I want to do this," I said slowly. I knew what I had to say. I just didn't know how she was going to take it. "But I have conditions."

Meg moved to sit beside me, her hands clasped together in her lap. She looked calm and reasonable, at least. "Which are?"

"You can't kiss me again." Blunt, but the truth. "I can't... If we're going to do this, it has to be as friends. Nothing more."

"Nothing romantic, you mean." She was still calm. Too calm.

"Yes," I said firmly, and waited for the backlash.

"Because you don't want more?" Meg asked, but she already knew the answer. I could see it in her face.

There was no point lying to her. I couldn't admit how much I wanted more, either. Not when we were giving it up forever.

"Because it won't work."

"You mean you're scared," she said. "I'm sorry. That's not a good enough reason."

Megan

He wanted this as much as I did – not just the marriage but the relationship. I knew it. The way he looked at me, the way he'd kissed me...

So why was he trying to hide it? What was he so afraid of?

Elliott sprung to his feet, his hands in his pockets as he paced the length of the aisle. "You want more reasons? Fine. How about this? We're getting married, Megan."

"That's not usually a reason *not* to kiss, El," I joked, trying to lighten the mood, but he just scowled.

"We're going to be living together, every day. Because that's the only way we can both get the future we want."

"I *do* remember the plan."

"Do you?" he asked. "Because this wasn't part of it. Friends only – that was the deal."

"Well, maybe the deal changed!" *Why* was he so unwilling to go after what he wanted? I'd held off this long because I didn't want him to back out. But now we were here … why couldn't we have everything?

"And if it changed once it can change again." Elliott sank down to sit on the chair in front of me. "Think about it, Meg. Your feelings about me have already evolved since the night you proposed. What if they shift again? What if we start dating then you meet someone else when we get to London? What happens to me then? If we fight, fall out – you'll kick me out and I'll have nothing. Nowhere to live, no friends in the city, no way to afford my degree *and* rent. You could take all that away from me in a heartbeat. That's why we have to keep to the arrangement."

My head reeled. "You think I'd do that to you?"

Elliott shook his head. "No. Not now. But … you don't know how awful people can be to each other when a relationship ends. How someone you thought you could trust, could love, can turn into someone else completely."

Elliott had seen it. He'd lived with the fallout from it. And he was going to use that as a reason not to go after what he wanted. What *we* wanted.

Because I didn't just want a kiss. I wanted him. And because he couldn't trust me, he was going to end us before we could even begin.

"You're wrong," I told him. "And more than that, you're a coward. This is about your dad. He's left you so scared that people – that *life* – will let you down, you won't even try and go for what you want. Can't you just go with the flow and enjoy life for a minute?"

"If I went with the flow I'd still be in St Evaline," Elliott snapped. "Probably planning on spending the rest of my life with Amy. Exactly where I expected to be before you reminded me of all the dreams I used to have – the ones I'd given up on. So I took a chance, Meg. I took a chance on *you*." The accusation in his eyes stung. But I couldn't give up, not now.

"Take another one." I reached across the space between us and took his hand, my heart pounding.

For a moment, I thought he might do it.

But then he looked down for a second and pulled away. I could see him mentally putting distance between us. But I still wasn't prepared for what he said next.

"Take a chance. You mean like Lizzie did." His words hit me so hard I lost my breath. "She wanted to be more like you, remember? She took a chance."

"You can't..." I shook my head. "You're not bringing my sister into this."

"Why not?" Elliott asked. "You think this is all about my dad? What about Lizzie? Didn't this all start because you were scared you couldn't live up to her memory?"

I wanted to deny it but I couldn't. I *was* scared. Scared that I wouldn't ever be able to step out of the shadow of her death and become myself.

"You told me all I needed was to be myself," I said, looking him dead in the eye. I knew he was remembering the moment when he'd said that. The way it had felt to lie there so close. "Well, this is me. Megan, not Lizzie. And I'm telling you, we could have something great together. And fine, maybe it won't last forever. But it would be real and it would be us and I believe it would be worth it. All you have to do is say yes."

Elliott looked away. "I can't."

I stood up, anger and disappointment pulsing through me. "You're a coward."

"Maybe. But it's my choice to make." He sounded angry.

"I'm not—"

"Yes, you are. I told you what this needed to be,

what I wanted, why I wanted it and you wouldn't listen. You only thought about what you wanted, not what it would mean for me. As always." He sighed. "Be honest, this whole plan was never about me. I was just convenient. And you knew you could use me to get what *you* wanted. That was all."

"We both get what we want if we go through with this," I snapped. Except we didn't. Not any more. Not now we both knew we wanted more. "Don't pretend you're not in this for your own gain."

"I am. But I'm not the one trying to change the rules."

Behind me, the door opened and the registrar appeared, flanked by Jade and Phoenix. "Sorry to interrupt, but if you're ready...?"

I nodded, smoothing down my dress as I stepped away from Elliott. Time to do this. But then Elliot caught my arm and tugged me back to face him.

"Come on, Meg," he whispered. "Marry me now and we can move to London, have everything we planned. But that's it, OK?"

"Or?"

He shook his head. "I don't think there is an 'or'."

But he was wrong, I realized as I stood there, watching the registrar prepare. The answer was right there in his words. Last chance. If I said no, we'd go back to St Evaline. And we wouldn't have London but maybe we'd have a chance at something else...

I hesitated, imagining a future where I could kiss Elliott whenever I wanted. But that wouldn't just mean giving up on my dreams – I'd be taking his away, too.

What would Lizzie do? Except that wasn't the right question. The only question that mattered now was, *What would* Megan *do?*

It all came down to who I wanted to be. Was I the girl who ran away? Who got married and kept running – away from my parents, my home? If I married him, would I be running from my feelings for Elliott forever – when I'd only just found the courage to admit to them at all?

"Come on," Elliot said. "Let's do this."

I wanted to tell him to stop, to let me think some more. But the registrar was waiting and Jade handed me the bouquet she'd bought for me at the service station, while Phoenix went to stand beside Elliott and grinned encouragingly at me.

I took a step down the aisle.

And then the door opened again.

BECCA
Sean, are you there yet?
What's happening?

BECCA
Meg, what's happening there!?!? Did Sean get there?
What about your parents? Did your phone die? Can
you even read this...???

BECCA
Elliott, your brother is on his way. Did he make it
yet? What's happening? Why is no one answering
their phones??

Elliott

The registrar looked up as Megan's parents barrelled through the door. I half expected one of them to yell 'Stop the wedding!' but apparently that only happens in movies.

"Is something the matter?" the registrar asked, perfectly calm.

Mr and Mrs Hughes stumbled to a halt in the middle of the aisle.

"Megan. You can't do this," Mr Hughes said.

"Our daughter is only seventeen!" Mrs Hughes yelled at the registrar. "I absolutely forbid you to marry her!"

The registrar didn't lose her cool for a moment. "Megan and Elliott have completed all the relevant paperwork, fulfilled the waiting period and paid all the required fees. And as they are of age in Scotland – and we *are* in Scotland – it's entirely up to them whether or not they choose to get married."

Beside me Megan was trembling, tiny shivers running through her, as if snowflakes were falling on her skin. She didn't even look at her parents.

Then the door flew open again and Sean stumbled in.

"El, this is the worst idea you've ever had," he said, pushing past Megan's parents to get to me. "This is worse than most of *my* ideas. Come on, let's go home."

The registrar looked at Meg, then at me. "It's up to you two how we proceed," she said softly. "Do you want me to give you a minute?"

I watched Meg for an answer. The decision was hers, as always.

"No," she said after a few moments, shaking her head. "I'm sorry," she said, her expression solemn. "I can't do this."

Then, shoving her service-station bouquet into my arms, she turned and hurried down the aisle, her parents following behind her.

Leaving me with the registrar, a very confused Jade and Phoenix, and Sean.

Sean clapped me on the shoulder. "Lucky escape, mate."

"How can you say that?" Jade launched herself towards Sean, knocking over a chair in the process. "They were so in love! They were going to live happily ever after!"

"They weren't," Sean said. "Trust me."

Their words barely registered. Megan had gone. She'd left me in the lurch, despite all the assurances she'd given me, every step of the way.

"I'm so sorry," I said to the registrar, then smiled faintly at Jade and Phoenix to include them in the apology. "We seem to have wasted your time."

"That's fine," the registrar said. "It's an important decision to get right."

"Aren't they all?" And I had a lot of decisions to make. Like what the hell did I do next?

"Ready to go home?" Sean asked, and I nodded. For once, St Evaline felt like a refuge.

Even if St Evaline was the same as it always had been, I wasn't, not any more. I wasn't even the same Elliott who'd left there a day ago.

We said goodbye to Jade and Phoenix outside the gift shop and climbed into Sean's car, which had been parked haphazardly by the entrance. There was no sign of Megan or her parents. I imagined they were halfway to whatever boarding school they planned to lock her up in.

Were they really trying to make her like Lizzie? Or were they just wrapping her up in cotton wool to protect her?

I rested my head against the cold glass of the car window as Sean started the engine. My brain was buzzing with too many questions and there were no answers in sight.

I needed a new plan. One that didn't rely on Megan or anyone else. One that was about me – the Elliott who was an outcast in St Evaline, who'd broken up with Amy, who'd spoken to Dr Robert Forrest about why archaeology mattered, who'd tried and failed to save Lizzie's life.

The Elliott who'd fallen for Megan Hughes.

Suddenly relief flooded through my body. Megan had said no. We weren't married. And I realized now that was for the best because I don't know how I'd have managed to see her every day and not fall completely in love with her.

"Do you think it's too late to apply for that Navy scholarship?" I asked Sean.

He laughed as he pulled out on to the main road. "You don't want to join the Navy."

"I'm running out of other options."

"The Navy's not the right place for you," Sean said. "I get that now. You have to really want it or you'll be miserable."

I didn't point out that I was pretty miserable as it was.

"Were you really going to marry Meg, just so you could afford to go to university?" Sean asked, disbelief clear in his voice. "Just so you didn't have to ask Dad for money?"

"When you say it like that it sounds crazy."

"It *was* crazy. Thank God I got there in time to stop you."

"You didn't stop us." I lifted my head from the window. "Megan did."

"Yeah. Why was that?"

My head thunked against the glass again. "Haven't a clue," I lied. No way I wanted to go into it all with Sean right then.

Sean waited a moment before asking his next question. "So. What are you going to do now?"

"I wish I knew." I thought about my UCAS application sitting on the computer at home, waiting to be sent. About Dr Robert Forrest, who'd said he wanted me to apply to UCL. And I thought about Megan and the way nothing else mattered when she was kissing me.

"Want to know what I think?" Sean said.

"Might as well."

"I think you need to go home, sit on the beach—"

"In the snow."

"In the snow," Sean agreed. "Sit on the beach and

watch the waves until you figure out what it is you want most."

"And then?" Because knowing what I wanted wasn't the problem. I wanted to study archaeology. I wanted my mum to have enough money to be OK, even with me and Sean gone. I wanted not to care what everyone in St Evaline thought about me. And I wanted Megan.

"And then you find a way to get it."

"Simple as that, huh?" Sean made it sound easy. In the real world, I knew it wasn't. "So, is that what you're doing with Becca?"

Sean's mouth tightened. "We're not talking about Becca. Now put some music on and start practising thinking. Seems to me like you've totally forgotten how your brain works, this last month or two."

I shoved a CD in the ancient player, not really caring what it was, and sat back to stare out of the window at the snow.

Maybe Sean was right.

If we'd gone through with it, I'd never have been able to risk loving Megan, never been able to tell her how I felt in case it screwed up everything else.

Now ... everything else was already screwed up. But I wasn't running away from it any more.

I was going to find something to run towards. However

impossible that seemed.

After all, Megan never let impossible stop her. Why should I?

Megan

The car journey back home was creepily silent.

Mum and Dad sat in the front, not talking, not looking anywhere except the road. And I sat in the back seat beside my rucksack, watching them, waiting and wondering.

Wondering what they were going to say when this strange silence passed. What they were thinking. What would happen when we got home. And wondering where Elliott was right now and if he was OK.

After weeks of having an exact plan, knowing every step I needed to take to get where I was going, suddenly the future was a blur.

Who was I now? Not a Lizzie substitute. Not Elliott's fake wife.

I had no idea what would happen next but I knew I'd done the right thing. Even if it hurt to think of everything I'd given up.

Eventually Dad pulled off the motorway, into a service station. I was relieved to realize it wasn't the same one I'd kissed Elliott in, earlier that day.

Nobody said anything as we all got out of the car and walked inside. They headed straight for the coffee shop so I followed. Dad joined the queue at the counter without even asking what either of us wanted.

I wanted tea. And maybe a chocolate brownie. And for Elliott to be there.

I'd always known there would be hell to pay when my parents found out what we were up to but I'd expected that we'd be able to explain it to them, logically and reasonably, when it was already too late for them to do anything about it. It wasn't supposed to happen like this.

Mum stared at me across the table. I looked away, searching for Dad in the queue. Still four people back.

"Are you pregnant?" Mum asked suddenly. "Is that why?"

I blinked at her. "What?! No!" I said. "That's not... That's not what this was about."

Mum sighed. "Then what, Megan? What could possibly have possessed you to—" She cut herself off, looking over at Dad. "We'd better wait for your father."

I tapped my nails against the table as we waited, until I caught Mum glaring at my fingers. So I sat back in my seat, wrapping my coat over my wedding dress so that hardly any white lace showed. I wanted to get changed but I doubted my parents would let me out of their sight long enough.

Finally Dad arrived with a tray of mugs and a chocolate brownie. He pushed it towards me and I stared at it, unsure whether it was some sort of trick.

"Eat," he said, sounding weary. "God knows what you've been surviving on the last couple of days."

"Biscuits and wine, mostly," I said, around a mouthful of brownie. No point lying now. "And a sandwich."

Mum rolled her eyes.

"Why, Megan?" he asked, as I collected the last few crumbs on my fingertip. "Why didn't you talk to us? What were you trying to achieve?"

I sighed. How could I explain this to them when they'd never heard anything I'd said before?

"I'll explain," I said slowly. "But I need you both to listen. No interrupting, no questions until I'm finished. OK?"

"I don't know what makes you think you can dictate the terms of this conversation," Mum snapped, but Dad shushed her.

"Go ahead, Meg," he said. "We'll listen."

I took a deep breath.

I could tell Mum wanted to interrupt, often, as I explained everything that had happened over the last seven weeks but Dad wouldn't let her. I talked about Grandma Alice's flat, how much it meant to me, how I'd pictured my whole future starting there, in London, with my photography business.

"I don't want to study economics or law or history or any of those things you think I should want," I said bluntly. "That was what Lizzie wanted. That's not who I am."

"But—" Mum started and Dad took her hand until she stopped.

"I want to be a photographer," I said, watching their faces carefully. "And that shouldn't be a surprise to you."

Mum and Dad exchanged a glance.

I pulled my camera out of its bag. "I want to show you something." Switching it on, I turned the screen to the preview setting and set it up to scroll through the photos I'd taken over the last couple of days. Then I handed it to Dad.

"It's more than a hobby," I said, as they watched the photos move across the screen. "This is what I want to do with my life. I know I still have a lot to learn but I *want* to learn it. I knew that if I stayed at home you'd wear me down until I ended up going to university to study something I hated and photography would never be more than a hobby. So I thought that if I could inherit Grandma Alice's flat, Elliott and I could move there and get away from all this pressure."

I waited, tense, to see how they'd react. I mean, I hadn't gone through with it but I had lied to them, used up all my savings to pay for the wedding and basically run away from home. I wasn't under any illusions about how much trouble I was in.

Dad looked down at his hands, his eyes sad. "I just don't understand why you did it this way."

Something broke inside me and the tears started to fall. I wanted my mum to put her arms round me and my dad to kiss me on the top of the head like he used to when I was little. But it felt like the table was an ocean between us. Like I was adrift and disappearing out to sea.

I'd wanted to be treated like an adult. It hurt.

"I … I just knew I couldn't be Lizzie for you," I said, between sobs. "And I know how much it destroyed you both to lose her. But I can't be her – I can't be anything like as good as her." I'd yelled that I wasn't her, I'd snapped that I didn't want what she wanted.

But I'd never admitted that I was afraid I'd never be as good … or as loved, as she was.

Mum got to her feet clumsily and came round the table to wrap me in her arms. "We never wanted you to be Lizzie. Lizzie was wonderful, and we loved her and we miss her. But we love you every bit as much and we always will."

"And we've missed you, too, Meggie." Dad crouched down beside me and rested a hand on my arm. "Ever since we lost Lizzie … we were so desperate to keep you close… But we never wanted you to take Lizzie's place."

"I couldn't if I tried," I said, swiping at the tears on my cheeks.

"No," Mum said slowly. "But not because you're not good enough. Because you're *you*."

Me. Megan. Just Megan. Not an Oxbridge student. Not Elliott's wife. Not Lizzie. Not even a photographic genius.

Just me.

It took a while but eventually I managed to pull myself back together. Mum and Dad stood up and retreated back to their chairs, and I knew that − tears aside − this was the bit of the conversation that mattered. This was where we figured out what happened next.

"So," Mum said, still sniffing. "You're not going to go to Woolten. Or Oxbridge."

"No. Sorry." Well, not really sorry.

"And that's not because of Lizzie?" Dad asked.

"It's just not me." I was expecting them to try and persuade me, to at least attempt to talk me round. I had my arguments already marshalled in my head.

But then my dad said, "OK. In that case, tell us more about this photography business you want to start. What are the costs involved? Do you have a business plan?"

"What about training?" Mum asked. "Do you need some formal qualifications to boost your credentials when you're looking for clients?"

I stared at them. They stared back, waiting for my answers.

And I realized how unprepared I was.

"Um, well, I've made some notes about equipment and stuff but they're at home." A flash of something came to me – a memory of Elliott's prospectuses. I didn't want Oxbridge but maybe university wouldn't be all that bad. Especially if it could teach me more about the sort of photos I wanted to take and how to build a business doing exactly that. "My photography A level will help, of course, but actually … actually you can study for a photography degree. There's a great course at UCL, I think."

"You're still set on London, then?" Dad asked. I nodded.

"Which means you don't want to sell the flat, I suppose." Mum sighed. "You should, even if you use the money to buy elsewhere in the capital, you know. It's a really good deal."

"But it's your decision." Dad gave me a half smile.

"I'm just glad you didn't make the mistake of getting married before you can legally drink," Mum added with a shudder. "Really, Meg. What made you think that eloping was a better answer than *talking* to us?"

"I did try," I pointed out. "You didn't seem to hear me. You were so certain you knew what was best."

Dad reached for his cold coffee. "When it comes down to it, we just want you to be happy. That's all we've ever wanted. And if photography makes you happy…"

"Then I suppose we'd better find out what sort of grades photography degrees require," Mum finished for him. "Assuming you're not against the idea of university altogether?"

"I'm willing to consider it," I said. "Maybe I could study in London, live in the flat and build up my photography business on the side?" It came out as a question but I knew I wasn't asking for permission. I was asking for their opinions and that felt completely different.

"That sounds like a viable plan." Dad drained the rest of his coffee. "Well, I suppose if we need to arrange a trip to London to research your options, we'd better get home."

"Yes," Mum agreed, getting to her feet. "And then at least you can get out of that wedding dress, Meg."

I smiled and looked down at my silver shoes.

Dad put an arm round my shoulders. "Just promise me that next time you wear a wedding dress, you'll let me be there to walk down the aisle beside you." He kissed the top of my head.

"And not yet," Mum added quickly.

"No," I agreed with a smile. "Definitely not yet."

Sean

Decline

Accept

Becca: Hello?

Sean: Hey. So we made it home.

Becca: And? What happened? It's nearly midnight, Sean! I've been waiting all day! Did they get married? Did Meg's parents get there?

Sean: No and yes, in that order. But ... it's kind of a long story, and it's already been a really long day.

Becca: Right. And you're still mad at me.

Sean: No. Well, maybe. But ... no, not really. Can we talk properly? Tomorrow?

Becca: By text? IM? Or will you call again?

Sean: In person. Meet me at the Blue Fish Café? Tomorrow at ten?

Becca: Isn't the Blue Fish a bit public for us? Are you sure you want to be seen with me?

Sean [sighing]: I'll go anywhere you'll talk to me, Bec. Just ... be there?

Becca: Yeah. Yeah, I'll be there.

Elliott

I spent three days on the beach, just like Sean had suggested.

OK, not whole days because it was still January and it was freezing but at least the snow hadn't made it this far south.

So for an hour or so each day, I went down to watch the waves and think. And when I wasn't at the beach, I spent time wandering round town, trying to look at it afresh.

It wasn't a magical conversion – I still noticed the dirty looks some people gave me and I didn't exactly go out of my way to find Evan Roberts for a chat or anything. But I tried to make my peace with the town.

Especially as I knew I'd be leaving it soon enough.

I had a couple more days before I had to submit my UCAS application and I still couldn't bring myself to press send. There was someone I needed to talk to first.

And Megan was nowhere to be seen. Even Becca had

no idea where she was.

I was starting to worry when, on the third day of sitting on the beach, Meg suddenly appeared and settled herself on to the sand beside me.

"Hey," she said. "Sean's car managed to make it all the way back here without breaking down again, then?"

"It did." I paused, trying to figure out whether I should be angry with her or not. But I couldn't be. "What about you? Take the scenic route back?"

"Sort of." She stretched her legs out in front of her, the toes of her trainers covered in damp sand. "The parents and I took a road trip to London, straight after we got back."

"Really. It all worked out for you, then." I wasn't surprised. I wasn't even bitter. Things usually worked out for Megan, one way or another.

But this time, I intended to make sure things worked out for me, too.

If I wanted people to believe I was better than my father, I had to show them. I had to make it happen for myself.

Sean had wanted me to go with him to visit Dad but I'd refused. I didn't want him to have any influence in my life. I didn't want his money or his approval or his support. I wanted to seek out my own life, for myself.

Maybe one day I'd be ready to make my peace with

him, too. But first I needed to make my peace with myself and my future.

"We went to see Grandma Alice's flat," Megan said, bringing me back to the here and now. "Mum wanted me to, before I made a decision about the developer."

"And?"

"I'm going to sell it." She looked down at her hands, resting in her lap, and I saw something sparkling on her right hand. Not the ring I'd bought her – that was in my room, since Phoenix had given it back to me. But a delicately woven silver ring, with a square blue stone set in it. "I'd thought that I'd want to keep it, because so many of my memories of Grandma Alice were there, that I needed it to remember her. But it's been rented out so long … it's just rooms now. And besides … I couldn't imagine living there without you."

She glanced up at that and I guess she caught the surprise in my expression, because she smiled.

"Mum gave me this ring to remember Grandma by instead. It was her engagement ring."

"You and your parents are getting on better?" I asked.

Meg nodded. "We are, I think. They're listening, at least. I mean, we still don't agree a lot of the time but … they're coming to terms with the idea that I get to make my own decisions about my own life. And … and they know I'm not Lizzie. That helps."

I bet it did. Megan seemed more relaxed.

"So what decisions have you been making lately?" I asked.

"I've decided to apply for a photography degree. In London. I'll invest the money from the flat so I can afford to pay a deposit on my own place when I graduate but, in the meantime, my mum's convinced me on the whole student lifestyle thing. So, halls, I guess."

"Bit different from shacking up with your husband, yeah?" Almost a joke. I was making progress.

"Yeah. Probably less fun." Meg gave me a sidelong glance.

"Maybe," I agreed. "I thought you didn't want to go to uni?"

"I didn't want to study the sort of things my parents wanted me to study. But … we've talked about it a lot. And there are some good arguments for going… Huh. Would you look at that," Meg said.

I looked up, following her gaze, and spotted Sean and Becca outside the Blue Fish Café. Their hands were clasped together and as I watched, Sean leaned over and kissed Becca. Then Becca laughed out loud.

"Guess they finally figured out what they both wanted," I said. There'd been a lot of closeted conversations at the house over the last couple of days. I didn't know quite what Sean and Becca had decided but they seemed happy about it. And that was good enough for me.

"What about you?" Meg asked. "Have you figured out what you want?"

I turned my gaze back to the water, thinking about all the things I wanted.

And how one of them was sitting right next to me.

Megan

Elliott was quiet for so long, staring out at the waves, that I started to worry he hadn't heard my question.

Maybe that was for the best. This whole conversation wasn't going how I'd planned. I'd intended to start with an apology, for a start. To deal with the giant issue of me abandoning him, basically at the altar.

I needed to tell him why. But first, I needed to know that he was OK.

Everything with my parents was working out so much better than I'd thought it ever could. But I couldn't relax without knowing what my happiness meant for Elliott's future.

Finally, he answered me.

"You showed me what I wanted. I'd given up on those things until you came along. So, I want what I've always wanted," Elliott said. "Starting with applying to study archaeology at UCL."

"You're going to apply anyway? That's brilliant!"

Maybe that meant he wouldn't give up on me, either.

"I hope so," he said. "I've been talking with Mum and Sean. They've been helping me research some bursaries and scholarships and stuff. I'm going to apply for everything I can, and get my references and CV in order so I can try and get a part-time job while I study. And if all else fails, I'll defer for a year and get a job full-time to save up. But it's going to happen, one way or another."

"It will," I said, fierce belief in my voice.

Elliott shifted to face me. "I made another decision, too. Also thanks to you."

"Me?"

"Yeah. I mean, your elopement plan was basically crazy, but it definitely taught me something."

"Never go on a road trip to Gretna in January?" I guessed. Because that was better than 'never trust Megan Hughes'.

"That it's always worth trying to go after what you want." Elliott smiled at me.

There was something in his eyes, in the way he looked at me, that told me we weren't just talking about university any more.

"And what are your dreams right now?" I asked,

my words almost a whisper.

"I've been dreaming about kissing you again," Elliott said, and my heart beat double-time.

I beamed up at him. "You should definitely go after that dream."

Elliott leaned forward, pressing the sweetest, softest kiss to my lips.

I grabbed his shirt and kissed him back. Properly.

"I'm so glad I didn't marry you," I whispered. "I don't think I could have stayed just friends."

"Even if it gave you everything else you wanted?" Elliott asked, eyebrows raised.

I smiled. "Turns out there's more than one way to achieve your dreams. And this way I get *everything* I dreamed about."

"You've been dreaming about me, huh?" Elliott smirked.

Laughing, I pressed my forehead against his chest and felt his arms wrap round me.

"Do you regret it?" I whispered the words against his shoulder and felt him shake his head.

"No. I've done a lot of thinking the last few days, and I think … running away with you showed me exactly what I was leaving behind. And coming back made me realize that I had to deal with everything here first."

He pressed a kiss to the top of my head. "What about you? Do you regret proposing to me?"

"Not for a minute," I said. "I'd never have found my way to being me, without you."

Elliott kissed me again and I sank into the wonderful feeling of someone knowing exactly who I was and wanting me anyway.

And then I realized something: I had no idea what happened next. Would we both end up studying in London next year? If we got accepted, sure. And what happened after that? Who knew...

I didn't have it all figured out just yet but we had time. Time to dream new dreams and chase new futures.

That was something Lizzie would never have and I wasn't going to take it for granted. I couldn't live my sister's life for her. But I could live mine the best way I knew how. By being true to myself.

By just being Megan.

Acknowledgements

As always, I have too many people to thank to fit the pages of this book, and am terrified of leaving someone out, but there are some thank yous that simply have to be said. So, thank you to:

My husband, Simon, for putting up with all the chaos that comes from marrying a writer

My children, Holly and Sam, for being unfailingly awesome at all times

My parents, for always encouraging my dreams, even when they sounded impossible

My agent, Gemma, for her constant support and helpful advice, like, "More banter. Flirting is good."

My editor, Ruth, for seeing the potential in an idea that basically started as 'two teens elope to Gretna Green because … reasons'.

Lizzie Gardiner, for her incredible work on the design and cover of this book, bringing Megan,

Elliott and the landscape of the story together in picture form. Also, for having a great deal of patience with picky authors.

Team Cooper, for being the most supportive group of cheerleaders a writer ever had.

But most of all, thank you to my friends – my Megans and Elliotts and Beccas and Seans – who got me through high school, sixth form, university and all the real-world stuff that came afterwards. Thank you for always being there, even so many years later, whenever I have a crisis or a celebration or a plan that starts with the words, "OK, this might sound crazy, but..."

About the Author

Katy was born in Abu Dhabi, grew up in Wales, went to university in Lancaster, then spent a few years splitting her time between London, Hertfordshire and an assortment of hotels across the world. She now lives in a little market town not far from Cambridge. She has a husband, two children, a goldfish and far too many notebooks. As a teenager, Katy was constantly in trouble for reading when she should have been doing something else. These days, she mostly gets in trouble for dreaming up new stories when she should be writing the ones she's already working on.

www.katycannon.com
@KatyJoCannon